THE DEATH OF METHUSELAH

Books by Isaac Bashevis Singer

NOVELS
The Manor   [I. The Manor   II. The Estate]
The Family Moskat   ·   The Magician of Lublin
Satan in Goray   ·   The Slave
Enemies, A Love Story
Shosha   ·   The Penitent

STORIES
Gimpel the Fool   ·   A Friend of Kafka   ·   Short Friday
The Séance   ·   The Spinoza of Market Street   ·   Passions
A Crown of Feathers   ·   Old Love   ·   The Image
The Death of Methuselah

MEMOIRS
In My Father's Court

FOR CHILDREN
A Day of Pleasure   ·   The Fools of Chelm
Mazel and Shlimazel or The Milk of a Lioness
When Shlemiel Went to Warsaw
A Tale of Three Wishes   ·   Elijah the Slave
Joseph and Koza or The Sacrifice to the Vistula
Alone in the Wild Forest   ·   The Wicked City
Naftali the Storyteller and His Horse, Sus
Why Noah Chose the Dove
The Power of Light
The Golem

COLLECTIONS
The Collected Stories
Stories for Children
An Isaac Bashevis Singer Reader

Isaac Bashevis Singer

THE
DEATH OF
METHUSELAH

and Other Stories

JONATHAN CAPE
THIRTY-TWO BEDFORD SQUARE LONDON

First published in Great Britain 1988
Copyright © 1971, 1974, 1978, 1983, 1985, 1986, 1988 by
Isaac Bashevis Singer
Jonathan Cape Ltd, 32 Bedford Square, London WC1B 3EL

Published by arrangement with
Farrar, Straus & Giroux Inc.,
19 Union Square West, New York, NY 10003

A signed first edition of this book
has been privately printed by The Franklin Library

Four stories were originally published in *The New Yorker*:
'Burial at Sea', 'Disguised', 'The House Friend' and 'The
Recluse'. 'The Bitter Truth' was originally published in
Playboy. Other stories first appeared in *Boulevard, Esquire,
Harper's*, the Jewish Publication Society, the Miami *Herald,
Moment, Northeast, Parabola* and *Partisan Review*.

A CIP catalogue record for this book
is available from the British Library

ISBN 0–224–02588–0

Printed in Great Britain by
Mackays of Chatham plc

Contents

Author's Note

WHENEVER I begin to ponder modern man and his disappointment with his own culture, my mind leads me back to the history of creation as it is described by the divine genius who wrote the Book of Genesis. The very creation of man became a disappointment to God. He had to destroy his own masterpiece, which had become corrupted. According to the Talmud and the Midrash, the corruption was all sexual. Even the animals became sexually perverted at the time of the flood, and perhaps later in Sodom and Gomorrah.

In my story "The Death of Methuselah," I explore this theme. Methuselah, the man who lived longer than any other human being, was madly in love with a she-demon I call Naahma. She and her lover Ashiel were directing a conference of perverts and sadists from all over the world. Evil had become man's greatest art, his main achievement. However, there is a spark of hope, because Methuselah's grandson Noah has undertaken the mission to save mankind from utter destruction, in his ark. This story was not planned as most of my other work was. It almost wrote itself "automatically." It told the reader and perhaps myself the story of cosmic and human art. Art must not be all rebellion and spite; it can also have the potential of building and correction. It can also in its own small way attempt to mend the mistakes of the eternal builder in whose image man was created.

All the stories in this collection were edited by my friend and redactor of many years Robert Giroux. Many thanks to him and to all the translators who have helped me prepare this, my tenth collection of stories in English.

I.B.S.

THE DEATH OF METHUSELAH

The Jew from Babylon

THE JEW from Babylon, as the miracle worker was
called, traveled all night in a wagon that was taking
him from Lublin to the village of Tarnigrod. The driver,
a small man with broad shoulders, was silent throughout the journey. He nodded and cracked his whip at the
horse, which walked slowly, step by step. The old nag
would cock her ears and look back with large eyes that
expressed human curiosity and reflected the light of
the full moon. She seemed to wonder at their strange
passenger, dressed in a velvet coat lined with fur, a fur
hat on his head. She even lifted her black upper lip,
which formed a sort of horse smile. The miracle worker
shuddered and murmured an incantation, which made
the driver realize how dangerous this passenger was.

"Giddyup, you lazy beast!"

The wagon passed plowed fields, haystacks, and a
spinning windmill that emerged, disappeared, and re-
emerged. Its outspread arms seemed to point their way.

An owl was hooting, and a shooting star tore itself away from the heavens and left a fiery wake behind. The miracle worker wrapped himself in his woolen shawl.

"Woe is me!" he groaned. "I no longer have any strength for them." He was referring to the netherworld creatures, the demons with whom he had waged war for a lifetime. Now that he had become old and frail, they had begun to take their revenge.

He had first appeared in Poland some forty-odd years ago—a tall man, lean as a stick, in a long yellow-and-white-striped robe, with the sandals and white stockings worn by Jews from Yemen and other Arabic lands. He called himself Kaddish ben Mazliach—a strange name—and maintained that he had learned the arts of clairvoyance and healing in Babylon. He could cure insomnia and madness, exorcise dybbuks, and help bridegrooms who suffered from impotence or from spells brought about by the Evil Eye. He also possessed a black mirror in which the vanished and the dead could be seen. He conducted himself as a pious Jew—on cold winter nights he even went to the unheated ritual baths, and he fasted on Mondays and Thursdays—but the rabbis and the community leaders shunned him, accusing him of being a sorcerer and a messenger of the Unclean Host. There were rumors that he had a wife of ill repute in the city of Rome, just as the False Messiah, the cursed Sabbatai Zevi, had had in his day. In whatever town he visited, pregnant women were hidden from his sight and the girls were made to wear double aprons, one in front and one behind, as a protection. Parents did not allow their children to look at him. In Lublin, where he settled in his old age after many years of wandering, he was not permitted to live in the Jewish quarter, or to enter the synagogues and studyhouses, but was forced to find housing on the outskirts of the city in a broken-down hut. It pained one to look at him. His long face was brick red, and the skin was peeling. His scraggly beard pointed in all directions, as if a permanent wind blew on it. His right eye was closed, blinded by fear, it was said. His hands shook and his head bobbed like that of a newborn infant. Scholars and cabalists had warned him long ago that he was playing with fire and that the powers of evil would not let him get off easy.

In the still autumn night, Kaddish curled up on his seat in the wagon beside the long shadow that traveled with him and mumbled, "An arrow in thine eyes, Satan, Kuzu Bemuchzas, Kuzu."

Born in the Holy Land, the son of a polygamous Sephardic Jew and of his young deaf-mute wife, a Tartar and a convert to Judaism, Kaddish ben Mazliach had wandered throughout the world with his cameos and incantations. He had visited Persia, Syria, Egypt, and Morocco. He had lived in Baghdad and Bukhara. He healed not only Jews but Arabs and Turks, and although in Lublin the Polish rabbis had excommunicated him and he was treated like a leper, he remained a healer and a magician. He had saved up a bagful of diamonds and pearls, which hung hidden around his neck. He had never given up hope that in his old age he would do penance and return to the land of Israel.

But luck was not always on his side. A number of times he was robbed and beaten on the road and his money stolen from him. He married several times, but the women were afraid of him and dragged him to the rabbis for a divorce, and he left them.

Just now, when his health was failing, the Evil Ones had begun to torment him and take revenge for all the times he had dominated them with his sorcery. For several years he had not been able to stay asleep through a single night. When he dozed off, he heard female laughter and the sounds of mock-wedding melodies, sung by she-demons and played on fiddles. Sometimes goblins tore at his beard and tugged at his sidelocks or knocked at his windowpane. At other times they mocked him, moving his possessions from one corner to another. They tore threads from his fringed garment and prayer shawl. Naked and barefooted maidens with braids hanging to their waists sat on his bed giggling, revealing their white teeth in the darkness. They stole his gold coins—he could feel their fingers slipping into his breast pocket. They twisted their hair around his throat as if to choke him, whining and pleading with him to give himself to them so fiercely that he fainted.

"Kaddish," they said, "either way you have lost the World to Come. Surrender and become one of us."

Kaddish knew that hordes of lapiutes were waiting for his death so they could grab hold of his sinful soul and tear it to shreds. More than once when he examined the script of his mezuzah, he found that the sacred words on the parchment had been erased. His cabalistic books were eaten away by mice and moths.

His phylacteries were cracked. Even though his hut on the outskirts of Lublin was heated, there was perpetual cold in the air and a cellar-like darkness in the rooms. To protect himself from theft, he hid his belongings in trunks covered with hide and reinforced with copper rings, all to no avail. No Jewish maid or housekeeper was willing to work for him. The old Gentile woman who cleaned his house hung crosses on the walls, and brought in a wild tomcat and a vicious dog. In order to avoid non-kosher food, he did the cooking himself, but the sprites and imps threw handfuls of salt in the dishes so that he could not take the food into his mouth.

Things were always the worst on the Holy Days. Toward Sabbath eve, he covered his table with a stained cloth and lit two candles in tarnished candlesticks, but they always blew out. He dreamed of creating pigeons and tapping wine from the wall, using the power of the cabala, but of late his miracles succeeded less and less. His memory had deteriorated so much that he had forgotten it was forbidden to kindle a fire on the Sabbath, and he began to smoke his pipe. The dog snarled at him and tried to bite him. Even the woman's little rabbits, kept as pets, had become insolent and crawled into his bed. It was no wonder that, whenever he was asked to perform some magic or healing or divination, he accepted no matter how far or how difficult the trip.

"I am lost anyhow. Let me at least save a single soul," he decided.

Now he was traveling to the village of Tarnigrod, to the rich Reb Falik Chaifetz, whose new home had suddenly begun to rot with fungi, and wild mushrooms were growing on his walls. Even though he was sitting up in the wagon, Kaddish was napping. His head hung low with fatigue, and he snored with a thin whistle. At dawn the sky became all aglow, and the road was obscured with a dense mist, as if they were approaching the open sea. The driver now walked cautiously beside the wagon, step by step, since people had warned him not to sit too close to the magician. Only when the mare made trouble—standing up on her hind legs and neighing—did the driver whip and scold her: "Calm down, old carcass! No horse's business!"

For a whole day Kaddish sat in Reb Falik Chaifetz's half-empty house, preparing the charms and amulets necessary for the purification of the dwelling's sickness. The rooms were damp and yellow spots covered the moist walls. Kaddish was sure that an evil spirit was hidden somewhere, perhaps in a kerchief with witch's knots, or in a cameo with unholy names, or in the hair of a mooncalf. As soon as he entered the house, he had got a whiff of the putrid smell. There was no doubt that the spirit of an enemy had lodged itself here, two-faced, unclean, and utterly vicious. Kaddish had searched in all the corners, holding a candle in his hand. He checked the chimney, the stove, and poked around between sooted cracks and nooks. He climbed the spiral stairwell to the garret and then went down to the cellar. Reb Falik accompanied him through the entire house. Kaddish set all the spiderwebs on fire, and giant spiders with white bellies slid off while his bluish lips were muttering spells. He spat on all sides where the unseen might lurk.

It was perhaps his last and most decisive battle with the Evil Ones. If they didn't surrender this time, how would they be driven away into the desert behind the black mountains forever?

Kaddish had come clandestinely to Tarnigrod. This is how it had been stipulated between him and Reb Falik Chaifetz. Nevertheless the townspeople had somehow learned of his coming. Even before his arrival, many of them gathered in front of Reb Falik's house. Women in clusters were pointing at him and whispering to one another. A few daring youths, climbing on each other's shoulders, tried to peek in between the cracks of the closed shutters. Some peasants brought their cripples, epileptics, their mad and their lame to the miracle worker. A mother carried her child ill with a seizure, its eyes rolling in their sockets. A father dragged a lunatic son, bound like an animal to a wagon. One woman brought a wench with a growth of beard on her face.

Reb Falik Chaifetz came out and admonished the crowd that no cure would come from all this. He begged them to go away, but the mob grew larger. Kaddish opened a top-floor window, stuck out a disheveled head, and pleaded, "People! I have no strength left. Don't torment me." He nevertheless received the sick and the lame all day long.

Kaddish was eager to leave town as early as possible. But suddenly the beadle came late in the evening and announced that the rabbi wanted to see him. Kaddish went with him to the rabbi's house, where the shutters were already closed for the night. The old rabbi was dressed in a black robe, his hat sat crooked on his head, and his waist was girded with a thick sash. He looked at the magician with fury, measuring him from head to toe, and asked, "Are you the infamous Kaddish ben Mazliach?"

"I am, rabbi."

"Your name, Kaddish, means holy, but you are unclean and defiled," the rabbi shouted. "Don't think that the world sleeps. You are a wizard who keeps company with the dead."

"No, rabbi."

"Don't deny it." The rabbi stamped his foot. "You conjure up demons. We will not endure this in silence."

"I know, rabbi."

"Remember, you will regret it!" the rabbi screamed, and grabbed his long pipe as if to hit Kaddish over the head. "For hundreds of years you will wander among devils and you will not even be permitted to enter hell. The world is not all chaos!"

Kaddish shuddered, attempted to answer, lost his tongue. He wanted to tell of the many people he had saved from death. He slipped his hand into a pocket where he kept letters from grateful patients, written in Hebrew, Ladino, Arabic, and even in Yiddish, but he couldn't move his fingers. He rushed out on shaky legs, hearing voices and laughter. He could not see where he was going.

He decided to return to Lublin at once, but the coachman now refused to take him back. Kaddish had no choice but to stay for the night in the empty house where he had spent the entire day. Reb Falik Chaifetz's maid brought him bedclothes, a candlestick with a thick wax candle, a kettle with hot water, bread, and a bowl of borscht.

The Jew from Babylon tried to eat, but he could not swallow. His head felt as if it were full of sand. An icy wind blew through the room, although the windows were shut. The candle flame flickered and shadows wavered in the corners, crawling like snakes. Large glossy beetles crept over the floor and a rotten stench was in the air. Kaddish lay down on his bed, fully clothed. As he napped briefly, he found himself in the cabalistic city of Sfat. His Yemenite wife knelt before him, took off his sandals, and washed his feet, drinking the water. Suddenly he was thrown out of the bed, as if an earthquake had exploded. All the lights went out. In the darkness the walls appeared to expand, and all the rooms rocked and rolled like a ship in a stormy sea. Bearded images with horns and snouts were pushing him, circling around like wolves. Bats were flying over him. Everything creaked and knocked, as if the house were about to collapse. As always, when the creatures of the night took hold of him, he opened his mouth to exorcise them, but for the first time in his life he had forgotten all the names and conjurations. His heart felt as if it had stopped and he could sense his feet turning cold. The bag which hung around his neck was torn loose, and he heard the gold coins, pearls, and diamonds pour out.

When he finally managed to get outside, Tarnigrod

seemed asleep. A bloody red moon glimmered behind
the skin of the clouds. Bevies of dogs who slept in the
day and prowled around the butcher shops at night
barked at him on all sides. He heard the steps of a multitude in a tumult behind him. A sweeping wind caught
under his coat, and he was flying. Lights seemed to
flare up, and he heard music, drumming, screams of
laughter. He realized it was a wedding and he, Kaddish,
was the bridegroom. They were dancing toward him on
stilts, calling, "*Mazel tov*, Kaddish!" It was clear that
the demons were marrying him off to a she-demon.
Aghast, and with his last strength, he managed to ex-
claim, "Shaddai, destroy Satan!"

He made an effort to escape, but his knees were
buckling. Long arms embraced him, picked at him from
all sides, tore at him, tickled him, kneaded him and
slapped him like baker's dough. He was the host of the
celebration, its impure joy. They threw themselves at
his throat, kissed him, fondled him, raped him. They
gored him with their horns, licked him, drowned him in
spit and foam. A giant female pressed him to her naked
breasts, laid her entire weight over him, and pleaded,
"Kaddish, don't shame me. Say, 'By this black ring I
espouse thee according to the blasphemy of Satan and
Asmodeus.'"

He heard with deafened ears a loud shattering of
broken glass, a stamping of feet, lewd laughter, and
squealing. A skeleton grandmother with geese feet
danced with a braided challah in her hand and did
somersaults, calling out the names of Chavriri, Briri,

Ketev-Mriri. Kaddish closed his eyes and knew for the first and last time that he was one of them, married to Lilith, the Queen of the Abyss.

In the morning they found him dead, face down on a bare spot, not far from the town. His head was buried in the sand, hands and feet spread out, as if he had fallen from a great height.

Translated by Deborah Menashe

The House Friend

WE WERE sitting in the Café Piccadilly, Max Stein and I, and our talk turned to married women with lovers tolerated by their husbands. "House friends" we used to call such men in the Yiddish Writers' Club. Yes, women —what else could we have talked about? Neither of us was interested in politics or business. I noticed that the men at the other tables were reading the stock and bond reports or the horse-racing results. The women were flipping through illustrated magazines with photographs of princes, princesses, murderers, adventurers, film actors. From time to time, they took out lipsticks and little mirrors and smeared their lips, which were already crimson red. Why do they do it, I asked myself. Whom do they want to impress? The men were all elderly, with gray hair on their temples. If they ever looked up from their newspapers it was to light a cigar or to rattle a spoon against a glass to signal the waiter for the bill. Max Stein, a frustrated painter, tried to make a drawing of me on a sketch pad, but without success. He said to me, "One cannot draw you. Your face changes every second. One moment you look young, another moment old. You have peculiar tics. Even your nose changes from minute to minute. What were we talking about?"

"About house friends."

"Yes, yes, yes. I say something and I lose track of it immediately. Sometimes I'm afraid that I'm getting senile. Men who tolerate house friends know exactly what's going on. They are not deceived for a minute. It is a real need. One day they get married and the next day the house friend appears on the scene. As a matter of fact, they anticipated his coming long before the wedding. These are people who are bored to death with themselves. Such men could only marry women with the same temperament and inclinations. Love is supposed to be an instinct, but what is instinct? Instinct is not blind, or what they call unconscious. The instinct knows what it wants and plans and calculates perfectly. It is often shrewd and prescient. Schopenhauer dwells constantly on the subject of blind will. But will is far from blind— the very opposite. The intellect is blind. Give me a cigarette."

"The pack is empty," I said.

"Wait a minute." Max Stein went out to buy a pack of cigarettes. He returned and said, "It looks like rain. When I was a boy of sixteen, I was already somebody's house friend. His name was Feivl and I was still called Mottele, not Max. My parents were poor, but Feivl's father owned a dry-goods store on Gesia Street. Feivl was always loaded with money. He went out with a girl by the name of Saltcha, and I was, as it were, the house friend. Every evening they went to a delicatessen for frankfurters with mustard and a mug of beer, always insisting that I come along. I used to ask him, 'What do you need me for?' And he would answer, 'It's awkward for me when we go alone. What can you say to a girl? I ask her about her home, her parents—this, that. But right away she begins to yawn. Somehow Saltcha has got accustomed to you. When you can't come, she makes excuses not to go. She must wash her hair, she has a headache, her shoes have suddenly become too tight, she has an errand to run for her mother.'

"One place or another, we always went as a three-some. On the Sabbath, after the *cholent*, he took Saltcha to the Yiddish theater on Muranowska Street and he always bought tickets for the three of us. I used to tease him: 'Aren't you ever jealous?' And he said, 'Jealous? Why? Saltcha just loves your company. Everything you say is charming. When you are with us she is in high spirits. She's talkative, she laughs, jokes, and she is good to me, too. Without you, she gets nasty and picks on me.' Once, I asked him, 'What will happen when you get married?' And Feivl answered, 'You will have to visit us every day.'

"And so it was. Saltcha, too, came from a wealthy house. Her father gave her quite a large dowry. The wedding took place in the Vienna wedding hall, and I was the best man. I had already begun to paint, and Feivl commissioned me to paint Saltcha's portrait.

"It was fashionable even in those days for a married couple to go on a honeymoon. Feivl and Saltcha's had to be delayed, for some reason, but when at last they were settled they chose Druskieniki—a resort on the river Niemen—and you won't believe me, but man and wife insisted that I join them. When Saltcha's mother heard this, she created an uproar. 'Are you all three going crazy? People have large eyes and long tongues. They will say the worst things, and you will be the laughing-stock of the town.' Saltcha's father was too caught up in his business to be bothered. As for my parents, they couldn't care less. I had already moved out, and there were younger children to worry about. We were poorer than poor and not overly pious. Besides, who cares about the purity of a son? To make it short, Feivl and Saltcha went to Druskieniki, and I went with them. Stop smirk-ing. What you think happened did not happen. At least not then. But I had already kissed Saltcha many times in Feivl's presence and he always encouraged me. If we met and I forgot to kiss her, Feivl would remind me. Wait, I will light a cigarette."

Max Stein lit a cigarette and continued, "There are men and women who don't know what jealousy is. They must share love, and besides, they never suspect anyone. My theory is that every human being is born with all his idiosyncrasies and caprices. Napoleon in his mother's womb was already what he would become, and so were Casanova, Rasputin, Jack the Ripper, as well as such geniuses as Shakespeare, Tolstoy—you name them. You may say that there are other factors involved—environ-ment, education, all those phrases of the sociologists— but the way I see it, everything in man is ready-made. Why do frost designs appear on windowpanes every winter exactly like bushes and flowers swept away by a hurricane? Why are all the snowflakes hexagons? They say that the molecules always form the same pattern. But how do the molecules remember to retrace last year's pattern? I have pondered these riddles from my childhood. In all my years I continued to make my own plans, but it always happened that I became somebody's house friend. I grew so accustomed to married women that when a woman told me she was single she became *a priori* taboo. Can you understand this?"

"One can understand anything," I said.

"How do you explain it?"

"One gets conditioned."

"Is that all?"

"If you insist, I can call it a complex."

"Well, you are a cynic," Max Stein said. "At my age that isn't bad, but at your age one shouldn't be cynical. Freud was in his own way a great person. The fact that so many of his disciples are idiots isn't his fault. All disciples are idiots. What were Tolstoy's followers? What are the Marxists? What are the Hasidim who wrangle and push to pick up the holy crumbs from the rabbi's banquet? What are those would-be artists who imitate Picasso or Chagall? They're a flock of sheep, and they're always driven by a dog."

"What happened with Feivl?" I asked.

"Nothing happened. Such people live out their lives in peace and quiet. He was a bore, and after a while Saltcha became like him. They had six children and all of them took after him, not her. When you told them to sit they sat, and when you told them to lie they lay. They

went to school and the Gymnasium. One of the boys
studied to be a physician. Another became a lawyer. It
was all perseverance."

It began to rain outside and it thundered. Night fell.
The daytime patrons gathered up their newspapers and
magazines and left. The waitresses took off the red tablecloths and the ashtrays and spread out white tablecloths
and silverware. The café became a restaurant. Max Stein
and I decided to remain for dinner. The crystal chan-
deliers were lit, and in their light Max Stein's face appeared yellowish and his hair white. He straightened
his tie and said, "Why creep around in the rain and
catch cold? We don't have wives and children. Since
you want to be a writer, I have more stories for you than
Scheherazade had for her sultan. I could have written
them myself, but I prefer a brush, not a pen. Besides,
many of these people are still alive and they would recognize themselves. I don't want any scandals. I have come
to one conclusion: that in life there are no rules. Beautiful women remain alone until they turn gray and wither,
while ugly ones nab rich husbands and have lovers in
addition. For years I was convinced that a woman could
run away either from a husband or from a lover—not
from both of them. But I was wrong. When I saw it
happen, I realized you can never be too clever.

"The husband was a dentist and had a weakness for
painting. All day long he stood at his chair and drilled
teeth. In the evening he was transformed into an artist.
He wanted me to teach him, but all he could do was
imitate others. He had a pretty little wife—Hanka, about

twelve years younger than he. For a time she was his nurse. Then she manipulated him into getting another nurse in her place, and when I began to teach him she, too, became my pupil. Things were easier for her than for him. He stood on his feet all day long, while she had a maid. Men are weaklings and women wheedle anything out of them with a smile or a love pat. He not only loved her, he worshipped her. Hanka this, Hanka that. He was dying to hear me say she had talent, and I said so, for his sake. She began to smudge one abominable canvas after another, and covered the walls with them. She ran to all the exhibitions in the Zacheta and the galleries and aped everybody. She read all the articles and reviews in the newspapers and magazines and babbled the jargon of the critics. Cubism? Let there be Cubism. Expressionism? Let there be Expressionism. All her heads came out square, and the noses as well. Chagall painted his Jews and deer flying in the air, and Hanka mimicked him. People of that sort are so greedy for compliments that they beg for them shamelessly, and if they don't get them from others they praise themselves to the sky.

"I started up with her not because of love or passion but because Morris—this was the dentist's name—actually maneuvered us together. At every opportunity he spoke to me of how rich the soul of an artist is and how difficult it is for an artist to become accustomed to one person only. Such men are not just tolerant, they push their mates to betray them. What Feivl did out of naïveté, Morris did with deliberation. He wanted me to sleep with his wife, and he got what he bargained for.

She also wanted it, to keep pace with the other artists who had affairs. It was the fashion with the so-called progressive element. She attended all their meetings, marched in their demonstrations, and ended up by running away with a low-life fellow—a knifer, an enforcer in the porters' union. This was something Morris and I did not expect."

"Where did she run?" I asked.

"Where did they all run?" Max Stein answered. "To the land of socialism, to the Communist paradise. It happened suddenly, like thunder on a sunny day. Little heads can be turned easily. She grabbed her things, left an abusive letter calling us Fascists, exploiters, imperialists, provocateurs. They ran to Nieswiez, at the Polish-Soviet frontier, and from there they smuggled themselves into Soviet Russia. The Polish guards let them cross without any difficulties. How they were accepted in Russia I learned years later. This was long before Comrade Stalin's purges and the Moscow trials, but even then they put them all into prison. While these slaves were falling on their knees kissing the socialistic dust, some Chekist or soldier of the Red Army appeared and said, '*Poidyom*—let's go.' Idealism is fine, but a few months in the Lubyanka prison was the ordinary reception for an idealist. I was told that all of them were finally sent to Siberia to dig gold."

For a long while we sat quietly, and Max Stein tried to balance a fork on the edge of his plate. The fork fell, and Max Stein murmured, "*Nu.*"

"What happened then?" I asked.

"What could have happened?" Max Stein said. "We were surprised and stunned, but how long can you be surprised and stunned? The first thing Morris did was rip her paintings off the walls and throw them into the garbage bin in the yard. I saw it all through the window. I expected someone to take them, but it seemed the tenants were not interested in Cubism, Expressionism, abstract art. They just stood there and gaped. There was not much time for Morris to brood. Patients had appointments and he had to see them. I heard them ask, 'Where is your wife?' and he replied, 'Out of town.' I still had a room somewhere, which I called my atelier. Since Hanka had left, there was no reason for me to remain with Morris and I told him the time had come to say goodbye. But he said to me, 'You, too, are running away? You'd better stay here.'

" 'What for?' I asked. 'To sit out the thirty days of mourning?' And he said, 'I'm not going to stay alone forever. Sooner or later, I'll find someone. I don't want to lose both of you.'

"It may sound like a joke, but I waited for Morris to get married so that I could again be his house friend. You're laughing, huh? I could laugh myself. Human life is not only tragic but also utterly comic. The room I called my atelier was small and dark. In the winter it was as cold inside as outside. I'd gone through a spiritual crisis a number of years before, and I had lost my desire to paint altogether. I certainly couldn't get a model to sit for me in that miserable hole. Morris had a comfortable home. It was light there and warm."

"Why didn't he marry his nurse?" I asked.

"This is exactly what he did," Max Stein answered. "Not immediately. It took him a few months to decide. Perhaps he tried to get a better-looking woman. Milcha, as she was called, was not a beauty. She had come from the provinces to Warsaw to study but without any means. She had taken a course in the Wszechnica, a folk university you could enter without credentials. I'll tell you something that will sound completely crazy. Because Milcha was a single girl, and not somebody's wife, I had no yen for her at all, but I knew that Morris would be forced to marry her sooner or later and so I developed an appetite for her. I started to compliment her, to praise the beauty she didn't have, and I offered to teach her a little painting. I even began to kiss her in Morris's presence. When Morris saw this, he confessed to me he had been in love with Milcha for some time. Love can be very practical, even made to order."

"How long did you stay with them?" I asked.

Max Stein thought it over. "A number of years," he said. "It's actually difficult for me to give you a precise answer. While I was with them I became a house friend at another home. I became like a yeshiva boy. I ate in one house and slept in another. You could write a book about it. I became such a specialist that when I met a couple and spoke a few words to them I could sense whether they were looking for a partner."

"People like that are all homosexuals," I said.

"What? These are just words, names," Max Stein said. "What people really are they don't know themselves. The fact is that we all are searching. No one is happy with what he has. A day after the wedding both sides begin to search, the husband as well as the wife. To me this is the naked truth."

Translated by the author and Lester Goran

Burial at Sea

THE THREE of them were sitting in a cell: Zeinvel
the Slugger, Koppel the Thief, Reuven Blackjack. All
afternoon they played with a deck of greasy marked
cards. Nobody had money to put into the pot, so instead
each one offered up his nose or an ear. The winner was
entitled to pull the loser's earlobe or pinch his nose. If
somebody won more than ten rubles, he could give a
punch instead of a pinch. The highest bet was twenty-
five rubles and a knock on the head, but it never came
to that, because losing could be dangerous. Toward
evening it turned dark in the cage, as the inmates referred to the prison, since the iron bars on the windows
were covered with a dense wire screen, and they just
talked and exchanged stories.

The subject turned to marriage, and Koppel the
Thief, a man over sixty, with a narrow pockmarked
face and a scar on his forehead—the relic of a knife
wound—said, "Not all men are alike. Usually, a fellow

of our kind will do his business with a female and then go his way. Who wants to get married? That's only for the straight ones. When you sit in this joint and your wife is free out there, she does just as she pleases. She can swear her loyalty on a Bible, bring you a package every day, kiss your feet, but you have no guarantee. For us, getting married is like a healthy man going into a sickbed. In Piask the thieves did get married, but the gang there had strict codes. If someone got nabbed by the cops, the others did everything they could for him. If his wife messed around and got pregnant by a stranger, she was done for. The father of the bastard, too, was made to regret it. I know. I lived in Piask for seven years, and it happened only once that one of their wives slipped. There was a trial and she was sentenced. She tried to talk her way out of it, but they wrapped a noose around her neck.

"Why do I tell you this? A thief, if he has any brains, doesn't rush to the wedding canopy. But strange things do happen, and sometimes they end up horribly. This didn't happen in Piask but in Warsaw—in Pociejow. Wolf the Whipper had his hangout there. Chazkele Spiegelglass was still alive. Pociejow was where all the brothels were. The streets were swarming with yokels from the provinces. Aside from Wolf's, the hangout for our crowd was a soup kitchen run by a widow, Sprintze Chodak. Sprintze kept kosher and wore a wig. She was a shrewd businesswoman. An only daughter was left to her after her husband's death. Her name was Shifra. This Shifra was the most beautiful female I have ever laid eyes on. She was clever as the day—not from schooling but from life. She spoke Polish better than the Poles and Russian like a native. And her Yiddish! A glossy tongue. You could kiss every word of hers. Her hair was red as fire, and she had the eyes of a tomcat. Her figure looked as if it had been chiseled. Whoever saw Shifra walking on a Sabbath afternoon in a tight dress, a hat with ostrich feathers, high-heeled shoes, a purse in one hand and a parasol in the other, could never forget her. Men ate her up with their eyes, but Sprintze protected her like a treasure. Before his death, husband and wife had agreed to marry her off early, and Sprintze had put away ten thousand rubles for a dowry at the Imperial Bank in Petersburg. The boys tried to trap her but to no avail. Shifra did the accounting in her mother's soup kitchen. She helped her buy food from the wholesalers. It was a pleasure to hear Shifra talk on the telephone. She bargained and she joked. I was then a young boy of twelve, but I lay awake late into the night and fantasized about her. When I finally fell asleep, she appeared in my dreams."

"Stop teasing. Get to the point," Reuven Blackjack said.

"Yeah, yeah. The point is that two rich men fell madly in love with her. One was the son of the landlord in the building where we lived—Mendele. He studied at the Gymnasium and at the Philharmonic. He always carried a fiddle in a case. When he walked through the streets, all the girls stared at him. His father, Leizer, had hired a tutor to teach Mendele the Gemara. There could have been no better match than Shifra and Mendele, but when Leizer heard that Mendele wanted

Shifra for his bride he began ranting and raving and saying that he would disown him. Shifra's father had been the driver of a freight wagon. Leizer's wife said to Mendele, 'My son, your wedding will be my funeral.' But Mendele stood his ground. He answered, 'I want to marry Shifra, not her dead father.'

"The other one who fell in love with Shifra was Boris Bundik, a practicing lawyer. He was fifteen years older than Mendele. He didn't live in Pociejow but on Graniczna Street, yet all his clients were from Pociejow. He was a big, handsome man, much taller than Mendele, and he was a friend of all the cops. It came out later that he had a wife somewhere, but in Pociejow he was considered an old bachelor. Sprintze was a client of his, and he used to go to the soup kitchen to grab a bite. They only called it a soup kitchen. It was like a regular restaurant. If she were paid for it, Sprintze could have cooked for an emperor. It became clear that Boris Bundik was coming not to eat but to steal a glance at Shifra. To sum it up, he fell in love. He wanted to marry Shifra, but she had already got tangled up with Mendele. The competition between them was fierce, and Shifra supposedly said, 'I don't know who to choose—I love both of you.'

"What I tell you now was discovered later. They discussed it for a long while, confiding secrets back and forth, until the three of them settled on a plan: since she loved both, she should marry both. It so happened that at this time Sprintze became ill with kidney stones and had to go to the hospital for an operation. Afterward she went for a month to Otwock for the fresh air. Shifra took over the entire household and business. Boris and Mendele came to Shifra and sat with her until late at night. People in Pociejow became suspicious, but Shifra was not one to let others spit into her kasha. If a drunk made a scene, she took him by the collar and threw him right into the gutter. Well, and who wanted to start up with Boris Bundik? They shuddered before his very breath.

"I will make it short. One day all three—Shifra, Mendele, and Boris Bundik—disappeared. Sprintze, who was back home now, woke up in the morning and there was no Shifra. She began screaming, frantically looking for her, but Shifra had skipped town. So had Mendele. There was an outcry in Pociejow. The police wrote out a protocol, but this was all they could do. Initially, people thought that Shifra had run off with Mendele alone. Later we heard that Boris Bundik had also vanished. The commissar from the police station was said to have sent out a missing-persons alert, but by then all three had crossed the border."

Koppel paused. He wiped his mouth with his sleeve and scratched the scar on his forehead.

"This is some story!" Zeinvel the Slugger said. Zeinvel was small, and round like a barrel. They called him Slugger because he had once smashed an oak table with his fist and broken all four of its legs.

"Where did they get married? In Warsaw?" Reuven Blackjack asked. Reuven Blackjack was the brains of the group. He wrote letters from jail for Koppel and Zeinvel. He had begun his career as a gambler, and he used to cheat the yokels at blackjack. Now he was serving time for forging a promissory note.

For a while all three were silent. Then Koppel continued: "Be patient. The whole truth came out months later. Yes, they were married in Warsaw. Before one rabbi, Boris Bundik played the role of Shifra's older brother and Mendele was the bridegroom. With another rabbi, Boris was the bridegroom and Mendele Shifra's younger brother. What does a rabbi know? You give him three rubles and he writes out a marriage contract. You could get married in Warsaw ten times and a rooster would not crow.

"How long can you tear your hair and curse the day you were born? Mendele's parents had six other children, and grandchildren, too. Mendele was the youngest. Sprintze cried and grew desperate, but in a soup kitchen you must be up at five in the morning and prepare huge kettles of food. Sprintze took on a maid, a cook, but you know what they say—'A stranger's hands are good only for poking fire.' Weeks passed. Months. Sprintze went to consult Max Blotnik, a wizard who claimed to be able to show missing people in a black mirror, but it was all hocus-pocus.

"One day, when Mendele's mother went with her maid to Ulrich's Bazaar, she heard someone yelling 'Mama! Mama!' She turned, and there stood Mendele, white as a corpse, in torn clothes. A tumult arose and she hollered, 'My God! Where have you been?' 'In America,' he answered. 'In America, and you are back?' she screamed, and he said, 'They deported me!'

"It turned out that the three had smuggled themselves

over the border to Prussia and had gone to Hamburg. None of them had a passport, but in a foreign country you need nothing aside from money. Boris was loaded, but Mendele got only a small allowance from his father. He could hardly scrape together a hundred rubles. Shifra had her dresses and a bracelet that was supposed to be gold inset with diamonds, but when she took it to a jeweler he said it was only tin and glass beads. When Boris Bundik saw that he was the rich man and Mendele a pauper, he began to show what a pig he was. For himself and for Shifra he bought first-class tickets to New York, and for Mendele a third-class ticket. Everything would have gone smoothly except that Shifra refused to be separated from Mendele on the ship. She raised hell, but Boris got his way. He had apparently had a change of heart about the whole dirty business. Why did he need a young boy for a partner? This kind of nonsense doesn't last long. You sober up and the game is over.

"Later, Mendele told the whole story to everyone. He was lying in a hole between decks and Shifra came to visit him from the first-class cabin. They ate potatoes in their skins with brine from herring, and she slept with him on a hard bench. Boris Bundik called her back to the fancy cabin, but Shifra said, 'Since you are so mean and stingy, I don't want you for a husband. As soon as we arrive in New York, I will divorce you. I want one God and one husband.' A fight broke out between the two men, but what chance did Mendele have? Boris Bundik had the paws of a murderer. He gave Mendele one slap and he spun around three times. Boris also attacked Shifra. It all happened quickly. Mad with rage, Boris grabbed a knife and stabbed Shifra in the left breast, straight into the heart. They tried to revive her, but she died on the spot. Some of the stronger passengers ganged up on Boris. They threw him down and beat him. The captain soon found out and arrived with his crew. Some said they should stuff the murderer into a sack and throw him overboard. Others argued that this couldn't be done without a trial. A sailor brought a rope and they tied the brute up and dragged him down into the baggage hold, which teemed with rats. He was to be kept on bread and water. A ship is not allowed to carry corpses, so they wrapped Shifra in a bedsheet for a shroud and lowered her into the sea. One passenger, a religious Jew, recited the holy words and the Kaddish. Passengers of all classes came to the burial, if you can call it a burial. Mendele fell into a delirium, banging his head against the wall. He was completely covered with blood. He could not even attend the ceremony. They carried him to the infirmary, where there was a doctor and a supply of medicines, and they bandaged him up and laid him on a bunk. I know all this because I heard Mendele tell the whole story—not once but many times. When Mendele got better, one of the captain's men came to him and took him in for questioning. Mendele told everything exactly as it was and left out nothing. Both of them had loved her, and so both of them had married her. They also took Boris to a hearing, but he denied everything. According to him, he was Shifra's husband and Mendele had tried to steal away his wife.

"When the ship docked in America, the captain went to the authorities with the whole story. There is an island there called Ellis Island—the island of tears, as the passengers called it—where all the third-class passengers were held. A doctor examined each and every passenger, and if someone had weak eyes or a scab, or whatever, he was sent back. The officials on the island spoke every language—English, Yiddish, Russian, Polish, even Chinese—and they took Mendele and Boris Bundik in for another hearing. There were also witnesses. Mendele again related the entire truth, but Boris Bundik lied through his teeth to cover himself. The officials on the island were no fools. They got hold of Shifra's two wedding contracts. One was signed with Boris's name and the other with Mendele's. After some time, it was decided to deport Mendele to Hamburg and to keep Boris for sentencing in America. There a murderer is made to sit in an electric chair and they roast him to coal. Mendele was never told what happened to Boris."

"Why couldn't Mendele stay in America?" Zeinvel asked.

"Because bigamy is forbidden in America, too," Koppel answered.

"He could have argued that he was the husband and Boris the lover," Reuven Blackjack said.

Koppel laughed, and winked. "First, he didn't have your conniving little brain. Second, what good would America do him without Shifra? There he would have to press trousers. In Warsaw he had a rich father."

"Yes, true."

"What happened to him? Did he remarry?" Zeinvel asked.

"Yes, four years later," Koppel answered. "The first few months he roamed around like a man without a head. He didn't want to eat, and his mother dragged him to doctors. He wandered through the streets and talked to himself like a madman. They wrote the story up in the newspapers. Not only the Yiddish but also the Polish papers."

"Did you know his new wife?" Reuven Blackjack asked.

"Yes, I knew her. A girl from a wealthy home, but she was not Shifra."

"Did anyone hear anything about Boris Bundik?"

"Disappeared like a stone in water."

It became quiet among the prisoners, and they could hear from outside the rumbling of a tram on its rails. A spark flashed on the overhead wire, and for a moment the cell lit up with lightning.

"Love is like electricity," Zeinvel said. "It flares up for a second and is soon extinguished."

"What is the sense of marrying two men?" Reuven Blackjack asked.

"And in ancient times what was the sense of a man marrying two or four or six women?" Koppel said. "Men held the pen and they made the law as they pleased. If women ever write the laws, they will make it legal for one female to marry a dozen husbands."

"Suppose something meshugga like this ever happens. How will a man know that he is the father of his child?" Zeinvel asked.

"He won't," Reuven Blackjack said.

And the inmates burst into the hilarious laughter of those who are left with nothing to lose.

Translated by Deborah Menashe

The Recluse

THE WINTER night was long and cold. The beggars
and wanderers who slept stretched out on benches in
the studyhouse began to stir and wake up. One sighed,
another coughed, a third one scratched his head. A
memorial candle in a candelabra beside the Holy Ark
cast trembling shadows over the walls and ceiling.

Footsteps were heard in the outer room and someone
stamped the snow from his boots. The door opened, and
a thin, pale man covered with snow entered. The beggars sat up.

"Hey, where are you coming from in the middle of
the night?" one of them asked.

"I've lost my way. I was heading in the direction of
Lublin on foot, but the road became completely blocked
with snow and I could not continue. It is a miracle that
I survived."

"In this blizzard it was more than a miracle!"

"You will have to recite the prayer of thanks on the Sabbath," another one called to him.

"You certainly must be hungry," a third beggar said.

"First I must drink."

The stranger took off his shabby coat and then another one underneath it. When he entered, his beard was white with snow, but as the snow melted, it became black again. He didn't really look like a typical beggar or a wanderer but, rather, like a merchant who had lost his way on a trip to a fair. He carried a satchel and the kind of basket used by yeshiva boys.

"What made you take to the road in such weather?" a fourth beggar asked. "You couldn't get a sleigh?"

"They didn't wait for me, and why should a horse drag me when I have my own two feet?"

"If you are hungry, I can offer you a piece of leftover meat that some good-hearted housewife gave me yesterday," said one of the beggars.

"Meat? No. Thank you."

"A slice of bread?"

"Bread, yes. But I will have to wash my hands."

"There is a washbasin in the outer room."

"Thank you. Later."

"Are you afraid that the meat is not strictly kosher?"

The stranger was silent a while, as if he were pondering an answer. Then he said, "To me, all meat is non-kosher."

"You don't eat any meat at all?"

"No."

"What do you do on the Sabbath?"

"The Sabbath is a day of rest, not a day of meat."

"What are you? A recluse?"

"You can say so."

"*Nu*, so that's it."

The paupers began to murmur and whisper among themselves. In Lithuania, a recluse was not such a novelty, but in Poland recluses were rare. One of the beggars asked, "And wine you don't drink, either?"

"No."

"What do you do about the four cups of wine one must drink at the Passover seder?"

"These four cups I do drink."

"What else do you allow yourself?"

They all waited for a response, but the stranger was silent. He paced back and forth in the studyhouse. He warmed one hand on the hot clay oven and walked to the bookshelves. He took out a book, glanced into it, and put it back. Nobody expected him to engage in conversation, but suddenly he came over to the beggars and said, "God Almighty sends us to this world to bear our sufferings. We can never escape from them."

"Who says so? The rich indulge in pleasures and enjoy life."

"What? I was once a rich man myself," the stranger said, "and it brought me no pleasure."

"Were you sick?"

"I was as strong as iron. And I still am, thank God."

"You speak in riddles."

"My friends, I won't sleep tonight anyhow." The stranger raised his voice. "If you feel like listening, I will tell you a story. I will not drag it out but get right

to the point. Maybe you can learn something from it.
Unless you want to go back to sleep."

"No. Let's hear."

The stranger mumbled something to himself and
seemed to hesitate. He again looked toward the bookshelves, as if waiting for their advice or permission. He
sat down on one of the benches and began:

"I was born in the city of Radom. My father, may he
rest in peace, was quite a wealthy man. I am not boasting when I say that I was a scholar as a boy and the
matchmakers were after me even before I became bar
mitzvah. I married an only daughter from the town of
Pilitz. My father-in-law was a rich man and he took
me into his business. Since my wife was an only child,
his whole estate was to be mine at his demise—in a
hundred and twenty years, as they say. We were child-
less, which was of course a misfortune, but what could
we do? My father-in-law dealt in timber, and, frankly, I
turned out to be a fiery merchant. I had all the other
merchants in the palm of my hand. If someone had told
me then that I would become what you call a recluse, I
would have laughed at him. My wife—Esther was her
name—did her shopping in Radom and sometimes even
as far away as Warsaw, since Pilitz was a small village.
She had a lot of jewelry, she kept two maids, and we
feasted on roasted pigeon and marzipan on weekdays.

"When there are no children, the man of the house
becomes the child. Let me tell you, I was by no means a
saint. I succumbed almost entirely to worldly passions.
For the sake of appearances, I studied a page of the

Talmud daily, but actually I did as I pleased. Of course I ate kosher food. In what way is non-kosher food better than kosher? I especially loved what others don't hate— you understand what I mean. I am by nature a passionate man, and one female was not enough for me. My wife was prone to illness, and two weeks in the month a woman is not pure. I traveled for business, and as these things will go, I often returned home just at her impure time. This caused me a lot of grief. So whenever I met up with an appetizing female I could not resist the temptation. I knew it was a deadly sin, but I found all kinds of excuses. The Evil One plays the role of the scholar quite well. He can turn and twist matters so that it becomes a *mitzvah* to eat pork on Yom Kippur.

"One summer night I was returning home in a wagon. There happened to be two passengers—I and a woman from a village near Lublin. There would be no sense in mentioning names. The night was warm and dark. The driver just happened to be deaf. Well, the perfect setting. I struck up a conversation with her. Her husband was a pious man—an arbitrator in rabbinical lawsuits, she told me. Usually I chose a housemaid, an abandoned wife, or some waitress in an inn, though I always preferred a married woman. For some reason, this time the Evil One got more than he bargained for. 'Baruch,' he said to me, 'don't be a fool. She's ripe for the picking. Have your pleasure.' I moved closer to the woman, but she did not respond. I told her she was pretty and clever and other such compliments, and then she slowly warmed up. Why drag it out? I sinned with her that very night, right there in the wagon. The road was full of rocks and the wheels rattled over the stones. As I said, the night was pitch-dark and the driver was as deaf as a wall. While it was happening, I was astounded, and wondered why the wife of a pious man, a Jewish daughter from a respectable home, would debase herself in this way. Although at the time I felt that I was catching the greatest bargain of my life, I had some misgivings about the whole thing, and the Evil One kept comforting me: 'Was King David given permission to marry Bathsheba? He simply sent the husband, Uriah the Hittite, off to war. *Nu*, and are all the other so-called saints really so good?' The Evil One has an answer ready for everything.

"However, after two strangers meet on the road and indulge in this sort of abomination, they feel ashamed, and even estranged. I sat in one corner and she in another. After a while, my eyelids became heavy and I dozed off. In my dream I saw a man. His image was as vivid as if I were awake. He was small, with a blond beard, dressed in a velvet gaberdine, with a wide fringed garment and slippers like a rabbi's. I had never seen this man before and I knew even in the dream that he was a total stranger. I noticed that on the right side of his forehead was a tumor. He came very close to me and said, 'Baruch, what have you done? For such iniquity one loses the World to Come.'

"In the dream I asked, 'Who are you?' and he answered, 'What is the difference? The eyes see only when there is light, but the soul can also see when there is darkness.' Those were his words. I shook and awoke.

I didn't know why, but his words stirred up a storm in me. I heard the woman fumbling with her purse and I asked her, 'Is your husband waiting for you at home?'

" 'Why do you want to know?' she answered.

" 'I'm just curious,' I said.

" 'Listen, mister,' she said, 'what is past is past. I don't know you and you don't know me. And that is the end of it. I will soon be at home with my husband, and you are on your way home to your wife. Let's pretend it never happened.'

"I had heard this kind of vulgar talk from loose maids, cooks, and the like, but coming from this sort of woman it was shocking. I said nothing more. I laid my head down again and dozed off. Immediately, I saw the same man, with the blond beard, the velvet gaberdine, and the tumor on his forehead. He screamed, 'You may no longer be called Baruch. "Baruch" means blessed, but you are cursed.'

"I shivered and woke up in a cold sweat. The woman, too, must have fallen asleep. I said something to her and she didn't answer me. Just as it is written in the Book of Proverbs: She ate and wiped her mouth and said she did no wrong.

"I returned home a shattered man. I had never before felt anger toward women I had had affairs with. Why be angry? But toward this woman I felt an aversion. Something burned in me and I didn't know why. I heard someone scolding me, but I could not tell who it was and what he was saying. I began to think: If a wife like her, married to a scholarly man, is capable of betraying him

so lightheartedly, then no man can really be sure of any
wife. If this is so, it is the end of the world. It also
occurred to me that she could have become pregnant
and would then bear her husband a bastard. I could no
longer rest. I began to fear that I had sunk into the
Forty-nine Gates of Defilement. I looked differently at
my own wife, too. Who knows? She seemed frail when
she was with me, but when I went away she might suddenly rejuvenate. I could no longer find any peace,
neither that night nor many nights and days after. My
distrust became so wild that when the butcher came to
our home and my wife bought tripe with calves' feet
from him I was already suspecting the worst. I imagined
that she winked at him and nodded to him. Weeks
passed in this way. Usually, time heals such disturb-
ances. But this restlessness grew worse. It was bursting
my brain. I was seriously afraid that I was going mad
and that I would end up in an insane asylum. For a
while I thought about going to a doctor and telling him
of my ordeal. I developed a terrible hatred toward my
wife, while I knew deep inside me that she was a decent
woman and such salacious thoughts never entered her
mind for a second. One minute my love for her returned,
as well as my desire to see her happy and well. Then I
wished for her death and I fancied all kinds of cruel
revenge. Whenever I saw her talk to a man, even if he
was nothing more than the water carrier, I was sure
that they were planning not only to betray me but even
to kill me. To make it short, I was on the verge of madness, or perhaps even murder. My good friends, don't

look at me that way. It can happen to any man if he doesn't curb the evil powers which dwell in all of us. One step away from God and one is already in the dominion of Satan and hell. You don't believe me, eh?"

"I do. I do," said one of the beggars. "In our own town a squire strangled his wife because she smiled at another squire. He tried to kill him, too, but he ran away."

"But those were Gentiles, not Jews," said another beggar. "And not a scholar of the Torah, as you seem to be."

"The Devil tempts everybody," another beggar said. "He can assail even the mind of an eighty-year-old rabbi. I heard this from a preacher in the city of Zamosc."

"True, true," the stranger said. "I didn't know it then, but I know it now. I wish I had known more of it then. My sleep would have been less tortured."

For a minute all were silent. The beggars looked at one another and shrugged their shoulders.

"Now listen to this," the stranger cried out. "One morning I went to the studyhouse and I saw a man with a blond beard, in a velvet gaberdine, and with a tumor on his forehead. He was greeted by the congregation with much respect. I asked who he was and they told me he was an arbitrator in rabbinical lawsuits from some other town. I felt as if I had been slammed over the head with a hammer. This was the man of my dream. I became white and began to shake. People came over to me and asked, 'Baruch, aren't you feeling well?

What's the matter?' I clutched at my head and ran out of the studyhouse. I went to my wife and said, 'Esther, take over everything—all the business. Consider yourself a widow.' She thought I had lost my mind.

" 'What happened?' she asked. And I said, 'You are a good wife, but I am not worthy of being your husband.'

" 'What have you done?' she asked. I wanted to tell her the truth, but the words would not come. She was actually not well that day and I was afraid that what I would tell her might kill her. To commit adultery is one thing, but to kill your beloved wife is something else. As a matter of fact, she looked as if she might faint dead away. Since I could not tell her the truth, I had to invent a lie—that I had some trouble with my business. She tried to comfort me. 'It's only money,' she said. 'Quiet down. Your health is more important to me than all the money in the world.' I realized in those moments that to suspect the innocent can lead to the worst of crimes.

"That night I didn't sleep a wink. For a moment I wanted to ask her forgiveness for suspecting her, but then I heard the Evil One say to me, 'This other man, with whose wife you sinned, might have acted just as cowardly as you if he had had some suspicion about his wife. They are all alike: false and treacherous. Before the Temple was destroyed, when the spirit of jealousy came over a man he could lead his wife to the priest and make her drink from the water of bitterness. And if she had really betrayed him her belly would swell and her thigh would fall away. But in our time they can give in to all lecherous desires and not a cock would crow.' Immediately my hatred toward my wife returned. I felt that I had to leave her. And this is what I did. I knew that to desert a decent wife was the worst thing a man can do. But I also knew that divorce papers could be slipped into her possession and then she would still be permitted to remarry. And I did exactly this. I went to a faraway town, ordered divorce papers from a scribe, and sent them to her by messenger. I knew that staying with her would be the death both of her and of me."

"And you never went back?" one of the beggars asked.

"Never."

"You were never tempted?"

"I was tempted not once but a thousand times. But I could not do it."

"She might have been pregnant when you left her."

"I knew she wasn't."

"Do you think that what you did was right?"

"No. It was wrong, but in the years I have been wandering I have heard so many stories of treachery that my faith in human beings has ceased forever. I came to the conclusion that nothing was left for me but to become a wanderer upon the earth. More than that, I never stay longer in one place than a day or two, so as not to develop any attachments to anything or anybody."

"You are always on the run?"

"I run from nobody but myself. One of my kind should not belong to any community."

"How long are you going to stay here in this town?"

The stranger thought it over. "I have already spoken too much. I will leave at sunrise."

Translated by Deborah Menashe

Disguised

WHEN TEMERL stood under the wedding canopy she
surely did not know that in less than half a year she
would be an abandoned wife. Temerl was the daughter
of a rich man. Pinchos—or Pinchosl, as her husband was
called, because he was small and slight—was a poor
yeshiva student. He received a large dowry from his
in-laws and was promised ten years' board. Temerl was
good-looking. Why would anybody want to run away
from her? But a few months after the wedding Pinchosl
was gone. He stealthily packed a few garments in a
bundle, took his prayer shawl and phylacteries, and left
the town on foot. Even though he could have taken the
entire dowry, he took only three silver guldens.

No, Pinchosl was not a thief, and neither did he chase
women. He barely looked at Temerl when he lifted the
veil from her face on the wedding night. Why, then,
did he run off? Some people thought he was homesick
for Komarov, where he had been brought up, and yearn-

ing for his mother and father. But even his parents heard nothing from him after he left his wife. Someone had seen him in Zamosc, someone else in Lublin. After that, there was no trace of him. Pinchosl had vanished.

People expressed all kinds of opinions. Maybe he had quarreled with his wife? Maybe he disliked the town where his in-laws lived? Perhaps he wanted to make an end to the Jewish Exile and return to the land of Israel? Even so, he didn't need to run away. He could have divorced Temerl, or at least sent divorce papers with a messenger. To walk out on a Jewish daughter is a grave sin, because unless she is divorced according to the laws of Moses and Israel she can never remarry.

Temerl sulked and wept. It would have been much less of a misfortune had he left her with a child. But he left her with nothing but an ache in her heart. The women questioned Temerl: "Did he come to your bed on your pure nights?" "Did he speak gently to you?" "Did you ever resist him?" From Temerl's answers it was clear that they had behaved more or less like man and wife.

As far as the family knew, the night before Pinchosl left he read a Talmudic book in the studyhouse until late. There was no sign on his face that he was preparing to do anything unusual. But in the middle of the night, as Temerl slept, he packed up and slipped away. Why? And where to? His parents and father-in-law sent messengers to look for him in the neighboring towns. The family wrote to rabbis and to community leaders across Poland. But Pinchosl had apparently managed to elude everybody.

There was only one explanation: the demons had captured him. But if the demons capture a man, he is not spotted in Zamosc and in Lublin. They drag him behind the black mountains where no people walk, no cattle tread. Some women murmured that perhaps Pinchosl harbored hatred toward Temerl. But how could anyone hate Temerl? She was a mere seventeen years old, with a silky-smooth face, dark eyes, and slender limbs, and she seemed to be utterly devoted to her husband. She had sewn an ornate prayer-shawl case for him and sent to him as a wedding gift a velvet matzoh cover embroidered with golden threads and with his name in little gems. If he dallied too long in the studyhouse, she sent her maid to call him home to lunch.

Rumors spread that a young man who looked Jewish had been seen in a procession of priests and monks at a cloister. But this certainly could not have been the learned and law-abiding Pinchosl. People often say that one cannot understand the ways of the Almighty. Yet the ways of human beings can be just as perplexing.

Two years passed. Pinchosl's parents and in-laws had searched far and wide. They inquired in every city or village where a Jew might settle. One day, Temerl surprised her parents by telling them that she had decided to go and comb the earth herself in search of her husband. Her mother, Baila, cried bitterly. How could she allow her nineteen-year-old daughter to wander over the world? Where would she go? Where would she stay? Baila was terrified that the same fate would befall Temerl as had befallen Pinchosl. But her father,

Reb Shlomo Meltzer, had another viewpoint. It was not unheard of for an abandoned wife to set out in search of her husband. It had happened more than once that the wife finally found the man and got a divorce from him or else located witnesses to his death. What did Temerl have to lose? Her life was ruined either way. Reb Shlomo gave his daughter money and sent along a maid to help her in all her endeavors. The maid, a widow, was a distant relative of his.

A long journey began for Temerl. She did not travel with any specific plan. She followed all possible leads. If she was given the name of some town that the messengers might have omitted, she found a vehicle and traveled there. Wherever she went, she sought out the rabbi and the community leaders, and she visited the synagogue and the studyhouse. She searched in the marketplaces, along the side streets, in the poorhouse. She asked if anyone had seen or heard about a certain Pinchosl. People shrugged their shoulders, shook their heads. Pinchosl had no outstanding traits. He looked like an average young Hasid. When he forsook her, he had not yet begun to sprout whiskers, but by now he probably had grown a little beard. Wherever Temerl and her maid went, they heard the same refrain: "Go look for a needle in a haystack."

Months passed, and Temerl pursued her search. Traveling all over the Lublin region and farther, into the so-called Great Poland, matured her before her time. She gained the kind of knowledge that comes from staying at inns and listening to all sorts of talk. She met with other abandoned wives. Men did disappear. Once in a while, a woman, too, disappeared, but those were rare cases. Temerl learned how vast the world was and how odd people could be. Each human being had his own desires, his own calculations, and sometimes his or her own madness. In the city of Chelm, she heard, the daughter of a rich Jew had fallen in love with a pork butcher and converted to Catholicism. In Jaroslaw, a wealthy businessman divorced his wife and married a prostitute. In Lemberg, they imprisoned a charlatan who had twenty-four families in twenty-four towns and villages. Temerl also heard many tales of people who had been carried away by hobgoblins, of children captured and enslaved by gypsies, and of men who escaped to America, where, she was told, it was nighttime when it was daytime in Poland, and where people walked upside down. There was also talk about a monster who was born with a gray beard and the teeth of a wolf. But Temerl somehow felt that Pinchosl had not been seized by demons, and that neither was he lost in faraway America, across the ocean.

Temerl journeyed through all the Jewish towns. The money that her father had given her ran out, but she had her jewelry with her and was able to sell some of that. She had written to her parents, but they could not answer her, since she never stayed long enough in one place. In time, the maid became weary of roaming and she returned home. For Temerl, wandering had become a habit. In one town, she met someone who resembled Pinchosl. She alerted the community leaders, and he was taken to the rabbi and later to the ritual bath, but certain marks on his body did not coincide with

Temerl's description. He did not have a black nail on the
big toe of his left foot, and he did not have a wart on his
neck. He denied having been born in Komarov, and
swore that his name was not Pinchosl but Moshe
Shmerl. He admitted that he was married and the
father of children but said he had not run away from
his wife. The opposite was true. His wife refused to
live with him, because he could not provide for the
family, and he had gone out to look for a teaching job.
The rabbi and the elders believed him, and Temerl was
sentenced to pay a fine of eighteen groschen for suspecting the innocent and giving a stranger a bad name.

Temerl traveled as far as the city of Kalisz, and there
she was passing through a marketplace when her eyes
caught sight of a woman who seemed strangely familiar.
Where have I seen that face before, Temerl wondered.
The woman was buying eggs from a merchant and
holding a basket, into which she put the merchandise.
There was nothing unusual about all this, but Temerl
stood there gaping and could not move from the spot.
Suddenly she realized whom the woman resembled: no
one else but Pinchosl! "Am I losing my mind?" Temerl
asked herself in bewilderment. She remembered being
fined the eighteen groschen for false accusations.

At that instant the woman glanced at Temerl and
seemed to be so shaken that she dropped her basket,
breaking many of the eggs. She attempted to run, but
the merchant ran after her, calling that he hadn't been
paid for the eggs. The woman stopped and began to look
for money, but her hand was trembling and the coins

fell from her purse. Temerl herself was about to faint, yet she noticed that the woman's cheeks were not smooth but fuzzy, as if she was sprouting a beard. Also, her hands were too large for those of a female. A wild thought ran through Temerl's mind: Perhaps this is Pinchosl dressed up like a woman. But why would a man want to parade around like a woman? It is forbidden by the Mosaic Law for a man to wear the garments of a woman, and vice versa.

The woman picked up the fallen coins and paid the merchant. She then began to walk away quickly. She was almost running, and Temerl ran after her, screaming and calling her back. The woman stopped short. "Why are you chasing me? What do you want?" she asked, in Pinchosl's voice.

"You are Pinchosl!" Temerl cried out.

Instead of denying it, the strange woman stood there, pale and speechless. Finally, she managed to ask—again in Pinchosl's voice—"What are you doing in Kalisz?"

"I'm looking for my husband. It is you!" Temerl exclaimed. "You left me an abandoned wife." In her dismay, Temerl began to choke and cry spasmodically.

The woman looked at her and said, "Come with me," and she pointed to a muddy alley strewn with garbage and pools of slop. There, after attempting to quiet Temerl, the strange woman admitted, "Yes, I am Pinchosl."

"Why did you run away? Why did you dress in a woman's clothes?" Temerl howled. "Are you mad, possessed by a dybbuk? What are you doing here in Kalisz and for whom were you buying eggs? Are you someone's servant or slave? Are my eyes deceiving me? Am I dreaming? Or am I bewitched? God in heaven, the terrible misfortunes that have befallen me!" Temerl began to sway and was about to collapse into a swoon. She clutched at Pinchosl's shoulder, and a horrifying shriek came out of her throat.

In fear of attracting attention and having a mob of people witness his disgrace, Pinchosl blurted out, "I know that this will shock you terribly, but I live here in Kalisz with a man."

"With a man?" Temerl gasped. "Are you fooling me? Are you joking? What do you mean with a man?"

"Yes, with a man. His name is Elkonah. We met in a yeshiva years ago. Here we bake pretzels for yeshiva boys. This is how we earn our living, and for this I went to buy eggs. Forgive me, Temerl, but I never wanted to marry you. I was forced by my parents. That is the real truth."

"Whom did you want to marry?" Temerl asked.

"Him."

They stood motionless for a while; then Pinchosl managed to say, "I can't help it, I must confess the whole truth."

"What truth?" Temerl exclaimed. "What did you do? Have you, God forbid, forsaken your faith?"

"No, Temerl. I am still a Jew, but . . ." Pinchosl stammered and shook. He again dropped the basket, but he did not bother to pick it up. He stood before her ashamed, frightened, pale, moving his lips but unable to utter a word. Then Temerl heard him say, "I'm not a man anymore—not really, not for you . . ."

"What are you saying?" Temerl asked. "Were you sick? Did some vicious people do something to maim you? No matter what you tell me, I am still your wife and I must know!"

"No, Temerl, not this but . . ."

"Speak clearly!" Temerl, too, was trembling, and her teeth chattered.

"Temerl, come with me!" Pinchosl both ordered and pleaded.

"Where to?"

"To my house—I mean home, where we live."

"Where is your home? Who is the 'we'? Did you find another woman?"

"No, Temerl, but . . ."

"Don't lie to me! I beseech you! In the name of God. Oh, I'm afraid!"

Pinchosl started to walk ahead, and he motioned to Temerl to follow him. As they walked, Pinchosl was saying, "According to the Talmud, when a man is overcome by the evil spirit and knows of no way out he should wrap himself in black garments and go to a place where he is not known and do what his heart desires. This is what we did, Elkonah and I."

They came to another alley and to a shabby-looking house. Pinchosl urged Temerl to come inside, but she refused. He pulled her by the arm, but she stood firm. After much hesitation, she gave in. Luckily, Elkonah was not home. There was a clay oven in the house and a kneading board. The place smelled of yeast and firewood. Temerl imagined that she recognized some of Pinchosl's books in the bookcase. A ladder led up to a

loft bed. Pinchosl invited her to sit down. This was no
longer the modest, bashful Pinchosl she remembered
but a worldly man who reminded her of the adventurers
described in the storybooks she used to read before she
married. Pinchosl offered her some of the pretzels he
had baked and a glass of soda water. He repeatedly
apologized for his sins and the suffering he had caused
her and her parents. He even joked and smiled—something he had never done in former times. Temerl heard
herself saying, "Since you seem to regret your sins,
perhaps you could repent and return to God and even
to me."

"It's too late for that," Pinchosl answered. "I can
regret but not repent. Those who are trapped in our
net can never escape." And he quoted the Book of
Proverbs: "None who come to her return, nor do they
reach the paths of life."

Shocked as Temerl was, she heard him out. She told
Pinchosl that there was only one redeeming act for him,
and that was to divorce her and free her as quickly as
possible. Pinchosl agreed immediately, but said that
the divorce could not take place in Kalisz, where he was
known as Elkonah's wife. "You could have done this
from the very beginning," Temerl reproached him.
"And spared me all the misery I went through."

"We know that we will be punished, and we are ready
for the fires of Gehenna," Pinchosl said. "Passions, too,
are fires. They are Gehenna on earth, perhaps the Gate
to Hell. Meanwhile, come let us have a glass of tea
together."

Temerl could not believe her own eyes. Pinchosl

served tea with jam for her. They were sitting and drinking like two sisters. He was saying, "My parents had hoped to have grandchildren from us, but certainly not through an outcast like me, who would be excommunicated by the Jews and hanged on the gallows by the Gentiles. But you, Temerl, will soon remarry and bring your parents all the joy they expected. I wish you good luck in advance."

"You are utterly mad, but thank you just the same," Temerl said.

That evening, when Elkonah came home—a tall, handsome man in a short coat and a silk vest, his black sidelocks curled in ringlets—he was told the whole story. While Pinchosl still spoke with the humility of a Jew, Elkonah proved to be like one of those who are referred to in the Talmud as profligates for the sake of spite. He denied the existence of God, of Providence, and the holiness of the Torah. He went so far as to suggest that Temerl should get the divorce papers from him, Elkonah, in order to save Pinchosl a costly trip.

Temerl asked Elkonah, "Have you no fear of God at all?"

He answered, "All I ask of Pinchosl is for him to come back soon and continue to bake pretzels for the yeshiva boys—some of whom I have managed to seduce." And he winked and laughed.

Some weeks later, when Baila was sitting in the kitchen with her maid, plucking goose down for a feather bed, the door opened and Temerl entered. It was snowing outside. An icy wind rattled the shutters. Baila let out a wild cry of joy and jumped up from her stool, and all the down on her apron fell off. The maid lost her tongue altogether. Even before Baila could greet and kiss her daughter, Temerl announced, "*Mazel tov!* Here are my divorce papers, written by a master scribe, signed by two kosher witnesses."

That was almost all she could tell that day and for many days, weeks, months, and even years after. The real story, with all its peculiarities, Temerl could not tell, because Pinchosl had made her swear by God, by the Pentateuch, by the lives of her father and mother, and by everything holy to her never to mention any details as long as she lived. All she could say was that she had found her husband somewhere and had got her divorce. The entire story was told to a rabbi and to the elders of the burial society many years later when Temerl lay on her deathbed and was reciting her confession, surrounded by her sons, daughters, and grandchildren, as well as friends and admirers from the region, where she lived to a ripe old age.

"There were many demands and temptations for me to break my oath of silence," Temerl was saying, "but, thank God, I kept my lips sealed until today. Now, after all these years, I am free and ready to tell the whole story, since the place where I am going is called the World of Truth."

Temerl closed her eyes. The women of the burial society had already prepared the feather to hold under the dying woman's nostrils to see if she was still breathing. Suddenly Temerl opened her eyes and smiled, as the moribund sometimes do, and she said, "Who knows? Perhaps I will meet this madman once again in Gehenna."

Translated by Deborah Menashe

The Accuser and the Accused

THEY ARE both in a better world, so I can afford to tell this story. One of them, the accused, I knew from New York. There are very few mystics among the Yiddishists. Many of them are leftists or former leftists. The Yiddishist writers (almost all of them are writers, one way or another) have a social orientation. But Schikl Gorlitz, as I call him here, was interested in the cabala and also in the wisdom that comes from India. He has translated into Yiddish the *Bhagavad-Gita* and the *Dhammapada*. He worshipped Gandhi. He was planning to translate into Yiddish the Zohar, *The Tree of Life* by Rabbi Isaac Luria and *The Orchard of Pomegranates* by Rabbi Moshe of Cordova. As far as I knew, he lived alone. How he made a living I don't know to this day—certainly not from his books, which he published himself. Many of the books he gave away. Perhaps he inherited some money.

Schikl Gorlitz never came to the literary cafeteria.

He was not the kind of person who complained to other people. He was small, a frail man, and it was difficult to try to guess how old he was. He could have been between fifty and seventy. There was a quietude about him and an atmosphere of spirituality, of one for whom religion, philosophy, and contemplation were the very essence of his existence.

Yes, he must have had some money, because he often made long journeys, mostly to India. Once, he brought me greetings from someone of whom I had never heard, a man famous in India. His name was Rajagopalachari, an intimate friend of Mahatma Gandhi and former Home Minister of India. Rajagopalachari had translated a story of mine, "Fire," into Tamil.

The other hero of my story, the accuser, was known as a traveling journalist. I met him in the fifties in Buenos Aires. I shall call him David Karbinsky. He traveled mostly in South America and wrote about his trips in the Yiddish press and later published his travel stories in books. He was a powerful writer and I once wrote a favorable review of his work in the *Jewish Daily Forward*. He responded with a long letter of thanks and with the usual writer's complaints about editors, critics, and even readers.

David Karbinsky was in his seventies when I met him. He was a tall man, and he looked remarkably healthy and strong for his age. His stories about the jungles where he traveled, the various tribes of Indians with whom he lived for some time, and of Jews he met in the most unlikely places enchanted me. How he covered the expenses of his trips was not known to me, because Yiddish newspapers don't compensate their writers for extensive trips like these. I knew that he had married children and perhaps they helped him financially or he had saved up funds in his younger days. In Argentina he once gave me as a gift the skin of a huge snake. I've never learned what kind of snake it was. Perhaps he told me the name when he gave me the gift, but I forgot it. The skin lay for years in my clothes closet in New York and then the cleaning maid threw it out. It was shedding too many scales. I was never a collector, and certainly not of snake skins.

May I digress? I knew a third Yiddishist traveler, a man who was looking for a territory for Yiddishists. He hoped that somewhere in Africa or South America he would find a country willing to donate a large piece of land for Yiddishists who would be eager to live out their lives with the Yiddish language. Of course, this was a sheer fantasy, because such ardent Yiddishists don't exist. There were many Zionists who at the end of the former century believed that if the Sultan of Turkey refused to give a charter for the Jews to settle in Palestine they should try to find some other territory. The fact is that the Turks did refuse and Dr. Theodor Herzl, the founder of Zionism, thought he had found a territory in Uganda. The Zionists all over the world became divided into "Zion-Zionists" and "Uganda-Zionists." It's a fact that Theodor Herzl died a Ugandist, and some of his former disciples considered him a traitor to the cause.

I mention these territorial projects because in my conversations with David Karbinsky I derived the suspicion that he, too, was looking for a territory for Jews. I really think that every Yiddishist traveler is possessed by a territory dybbuk. If there is ever a Yiddish astronaut and he lands on the planet Mars, I'm sure he will look for a territory for Yiddishists there.

Now back to the story. Who was the accuser and who was the accused?

The accuser was David Karbinsky and the accused was Schikl Gorlitz.

One day when David Karbinsky came back to Argentina from a long journey around South America he made an accusation that shook the pillars of Yiddishism. He called a press conference in Buenos Aires and he told the journalists that while he was visiting the capital of Peru, Lima, he saw a long Catholic procession on Good Friday. Hundreds of priests and nuns and other pious Catholics walked in this procession, carried crosses, icons of the saints and apostles, and sang religious liturgies. Among the priests one appeared to Karbinsky to be very familiar. He was small, somewhat bent, dressed in dark priestly garb, but Karbinsky was sure he had met him somewhere, perhaps in the literary cafeteria on East Broadway in New York. He was singing and Karbinsky was positive he had heard his voice before. Karbinsky began to follow the procession, keeping his eyes continually on the little figure of the priest, who looked to him not only familiar but like a typical East European Jew. Suddenly Karbinsky knew. The priest was Schikl Gorlitz, the translator of the *Bhagavad-Gita*, the cabalist who was about to translate the Zohar and other cabalist works into the mother language. Karbinsky called out his name, "Schikl, Schikl Gorlitz." The little priest turned his head but seemed to decide to ignore the call and continued his march. David Karbinsky could not follow the procession much longer. Thousands of onlookers filled the streets. He could not thrust himself into the middle of the procession to query one of the priests about his identity. He had to let the procession pass him by, but he remained convinced that, without the slightest doubt, the frail priest with the dark eyes and the face of a yeshiva scholar was Schikl Gorlitz.

When the Yiddish journalists in Argentina heard the strange accusation they couldn't believe there was an iota of truth to it. Why should a Yiddish writer from New York play the charlatan and who ever heard that Schikl Gorlitz had made trips to South America and knew Spanish? They all said the same thing: People sometimes resemble one another. But David Karbinsky refused to rest his case. He began to do research and he learned that Schikl Gorlitz did make trips to South America. He also had translated some religious poetry from Spanish into Yiddish.

While this news was becoming public, Schikl Gorlitz was on one of his journeys. When he returned to New York and heard of the queer accusation, he denied it categorically. He was interested in Buddhism and not in Catholicism. He admitted that he had made a few trips to South America, but between making a trip and being a priest in Peru is a far cry. He said that David Karbinsky must have lost his mind, or was conspiring to ruin his reputation. But why should David Karbinsky be his enemy? They did not compete professionally. Schikl Gorlitz swore that he had not the slightest idea of what could be Karbinsky's motivation.

I want to say here that if someone with energy had undertaken to investigate the matter it would not have taken long to establish the truth. The Catholic clergy in Peru certainly knew who was who in their parishes. Also, Schikl Gorlitz couldn't have made any trips without a passport, which often bears stamps of visas and dates. Schikl Gorlitz belonged to the Peretz Verein, the union of Yiddish writers in America, and they could have clarified the situation by contacting the Peruvian clergy. But Schikl Gorlitz was not the kind of person who would insist on saving his name from the accusation of being an imposter. He suffered his disgrace in silence. True, he was accused of being a charlatan, but he most probably thought that false accusations, shame, and slanders are a part of man's karma. He denied the charges once and returned to his work. Like anyone else, rich or poor, Schikl Gorlitz might have had enemies, but he made no further effort to deny his guilt. If I'm not mistaken, he died not long after. It is quite possible that this ignoble affair may have caused his death. David Karbinsky lived two or three years longer. Schikl Gorlitz left this world as quietly as he had lived in it. If he left manuscripts, I'm sure the superintendent of the shabby rooming house threw them into the garbage together with his few other belongings. How David Karbinsky could have made such an accusation and not tried with all his means to find the truth is still a riddle to me.

Suspicion has such an uncanny power that no matter how senseless and unjust it is, it can never be completely eradicated. I myself sometimes play with the idea that, who knows, perhaps Schikl Gorlitz was what Professor MacDougal called a multiple personality. Perhaps Schikl Gorlitz was a Yiddish writer in New York, a Buddhist in India, and a Catholic priest in Peru. Maybe he believed that there is no essential difference among these three faiths. Perhaps there was a woman (or two or three women) connected with these eerie complications. It could have been that Schikl Gorlitz was a member of a group of people whose aim it was to unite all religions into one world religion. So many impossible things have become possible in my lifetime that I've made up my mind to erase the word "impossible" from my vocabulary. I'm even capable of believing that Schikl Gorlitz and David Karbinsky have met in the heavenly spheres, where a court of justice was held and the truth came out clearly and definitely. Somewhere in the universe the truth must be stated. Of one thing I'm convinced—that here on earth justice and truth are forever and absolutely beyond our grasp.

Translated by the author and Lester Goran

The Trap

"I TRIED to write," the woman said, "but first of all I'm not a writer. Second, even if I were a writer I couldn't write this story. The moment I begin—and I began a number of times—my fountain pen starts to make ugly smudges on the paper. I never learned how to type. They brought me up so that I have no skill for technical things. I cannot drive a car. I cannot change a fuse. Even to find the right channel on a television set is for me a problem."

The woman who said this to me had white hair and a young face without wrinkles. I had put her crutches in a corner. She sat in my apartment in a chair which I had purchased some time ago in an antique store.

She said, "My father and mother both came from rich homes. My maternal grandfather was actually a millionaire in Germany. He lost everything in the inflation after World War I. He was lucky; he died in Berlin long before Hitler came to power. My father came from Alsace. For some reason my father always warned me not to have anything to do with Jews who come from Russia. He used to say they aren't honest and they're all Communists. If he had lived to see my husband he would have been surprised. I never met as violent an adversary of Communism as he was. Boris was his name. He assured me many times that Roosevelt was a hidden Bolshevik and that he had an agreement with Stalin to deliver half of Europe to him on a silver platter, and even the United States. Boris's father was a Russian, a devout Christian, and a Slavophile. His wife, Boris's mother, was Jewish. She was a Hungarian. I did not know her. She was a classic beauty and completely eccentric. In their last years husband and wife did not talk to each other. When they wanted to communicate they sent notes to each other through the maid. I'm not going to bother you with too many details. I'll come right to the point.

"I met Boris in 1938 in a hotel in Lake Placid in the Adirondacks. My father had died in Dachau, where the Nazis had sent him. From grief my mother lost her mind, and she was placed in an insane asylum. Boris was a guest in the hotel and I was a chambermaid. I had come from Germany without a penny, and this was the only job I could get. Our matchmaker was Thomas Mann's novel *Buddenbrooks*. I came to make Boris's room and there the novel lay on the table. I was in love with that work. For a while I left the bed which I was making and began to leaf through the pages. Suddenly the door opened and Boris came in. He was twelve years older than I. I was then twenty-four and he was thirty-

six. I'm not going to boast to you about my good looks.
What you are seeing now is a ruin. The woman who
sits here before you went through five operations. In
one case I actually died. I stopped breathing some hours
after the operation, and the night nurse without any
ceremony covered my face with a sheet. Don't laugh.
Those were the happiest moments I can remember. If
death is actually as blissful as those minutes were,
there's no reason to fear it."

"How were you revived?" I asked.

"Oh, the night nurse suddenly decided that she'd
better notify the doctor. A number of physicians ran in
and brought me back to life. What a miserable life! But
all the wretchedness came later. I can never tell anything in chronological order. I have no sense of time and
have no recollection for the order of events. Do me a
favor and bring me a glass of water."

"Yes, of course."

I brought the woman a glass of water, and I said, "I
forgot to ask you your name. Is it a secret?"

"No secret. My name is Regina Kozlov. Kozlov is
my husband's surname. My maiden name is Wertheim.
I will try to make my story as short as possible.

"We stood in the hotel room and we both praised
Thomas Mann. Boris was tall, straight, a handsome
man; perhaps too handsome. I told him that he could
have been a film actor, but even then I saw something
in his eyes which frightened me. They had not one color
but a few colors: blue, green, and even violet. They
expressed a kind of stubbornness, severity, fanaticism.
Why go on? We fell in love, as they say, at first sight,

and two weeks later we got married right there in Lake Placid.

"Neither he nor I had any close relatives in America. He told me he had a sister in London who was married to an English aristocrat, some sir or lord. What did I care? I was absolutely alone in the world, without means, and here I got a husband who had received a law degree in Warsaw. He told me that he didn't have the patience to take a bar examination in the United States and that he made a living from business. 'What kind of business?' I asked him, and he said, 'Stocks and bonds.' After the Wall Street crash most stocks fell so low they became almost worthless, but at the end of the thirties they began to rise. Boris had brought with him to the United States quite a large sum of money, and in some five years he had managed to double or triple his investments. In New York he had bought a large building for a pittance, and he sold it with a big profit. He had an apartment in Brooklyn Heights, stocks and bonds which may have been worth half a million dollars, and all he needed was a wife. 'How did it happen that the girls did not grab you up till now?' I asked, and he said that many tried but he had never found anyone who pleased him. He said to me, 'I'm a serious man and to me marriage is a serious institution. I demand from a woman physical and spiritual beauty and strong moral values. When I take one look at someone I can see all her shortcomings, not only the actual but also the potential ones.'

"According to his talk, I was at least an angel, if not a goddess, and he had seen all this at first sight. It's a fact that he began to talk to me about marriage im-

mediately in the room which I came to clean. To make
it short, one day I was a chambermaid and a few days
later I was engaged to become Mrs. Kozlov. The hotel
was full of German Jews. The announcement created
quite a sensation among them. They're not accustomed
to such quick decisions. Mothers of marriageable
daughters were bursting with envy. I must tell you a
funny episode: The first or second day he asked me if
I was a virgin and I told him yes, which was the truth.
I added in a joke, 'A virgin with a certificate.' The
moment I said these words Boris became tense and
frightened. 'A certificate from whom?' he asked. 'From
a doctor? What doctor? Here in America?' I assured
him again and again that I was joking. 'Certificate' is a
Yiddish expression that means one hundred percent.
But I could see that he did not have the slightest sense
of humor. It took me a long time to quiet him. I saw
right away that one could not make a joke with Boris.
If there was such a thing as a degree for humorlessness
he would have gotten one magna cum laude. We were
married at Lake Placid by a justice of the peace, and
no one took part in the ceremony but two bailiffs who
served as witnesses. Boris had a sister in London, but
as far as I knew he didn't inform her of our marriage.
After a while we went to New York. My entire luggage
consisted of one valise. Boris lived in a small apartment
in a building without an elevator: two large half-empty
rooms, a kitchen, and a little room which he called his
office. It may sound funny to you, but he had one narrow
bed, one plate, one spoon, one knife, and one glass. I
asked what he did when he had company and he said,

'No one ever comes to me.' I asked him, 'Don't you have any friends?' and he said, 'There are no friends. My only friend is my broker.' It didn't take me long to realize I had married a man who was pathologically literal. He had a book where he kept a record of every cent he spent. Once when I walked with him on the street I found a penny on the sidewalk. I gave it to him for good luck, and he later wrote down the penny as income in his book. I'm not even sure that I should call him a miser. He later bought me clothes and jewelry. He planned to buy a house, but not until I became pregnant. I would say that he was extremely serious, and the slightest hint of a joke drove him into confusion. I read some time ago that they're building robots that think. If such robots are built they'll be just like Boris: accurate, precise, practical, and pragmatic. In the short time we spent together at Lake Placid it became clear he was a silent man. He said only what he had to say. I cannot to this day say why he was so delighted with *Buddenbrooks*, a work filled with humor: perhaps because extremes attract one another. This man could have lived out his life with two words, 'yes' and 'no.' I had made a tragic mistake, but I decided to make the best of it. I wanted to be a devoted wife and later a devoted mother. We both wanted children. I hoped the children would take after my family, not his.

"It was a terribly lonesome existence from the beginning. Boris awakened every day at seven o'clock to the second. He ate the same breakfast every morning. He suffered from an ulcer and the doctor had put him on a diet, which he followed rigorously. He went to bed exactly at ten. He never changed his single bed into a double bed, waiting for the time when he'd buy a house. We were living among Jews. The war had begun. Jewish boys and girls were collecting money for Palestine, but Boris told them he was an anti-Zionist. There were also some Communists on our street, and they collected money for Birobidzhan and such similar fakes. When Boris heard the word 'Communists' he became wild. He screamed that Russia was ruled by murderers and vampires. He said that his only hope was that Hitler would clean up the red swamp. For a Jew to put his hopes in Hitler was a terrible thing. The neighbors all stopped greeting me. There was even a rumor that neither of us was a Jew.

"When five months passed and I did not get pregnant, Boris demanded that I visit a doctor. This was a bitter pill for me. I was always shy, and it embarrassed me to be examined by a gynecologist. I told Boris it was too early to go to doctors, and he fell into a rage. The idea that someone could see things differently from the way he did made him furious. I went to a gynecologist, and he came to the conclusion that I was a hundred percent normal. The doctor suggested that it would be quite appropriate for my husband to be examined, too. I told Boris, and he immediately made an appointment. He went through a multitude of tests, and it was established that he was the one who was sterile, not I.

"It was a blow for both of us. I let it slip out that perhaps we should adopt a child. Immediately Boris became hysterical. He screamed that never in his life would he take into his house a bastard whose parents were criminals and who would grow up to be a criminal himself. He yelled so loudly I was afraid the neighbors would come running. I kept assuring him that I wouldn't adopt anyone against his will and he needn't create scandals, but when he fell into a rage he couldn't be quieted. I must say sometimes his screams were more welcome than his silence.

"Actually, Boris carried on long telephone conversations with his broker. Sometimes they spoke for an hour, even longer. This broker was a private consultant, not a member of a brokerage firm. In all my married years I never met him. In the six years we lived together I couldn't get Boris to go with me to a theater, a movie, or a concert. He was interested in nothing but money. I must tell you all this so that you'll understand what happened later. Please be patient."

"Yes, I'm patient," I said.

We rested for a few minutes, and the woman took a lozenge and a sip of water. I asked, "What kind of a married life was this?"

The woman's eyes lit up. "It's good that you asked me," she said. "I wanted to talk about it myself. We had two exceedingly narrow beds. He never let me buy anything except food. He alone was the buyer and he always looked for bargains. No, it wasn't good between us, and it reached a stage where I thanked God when he left me alone."

"What was he? Impotent?"

"Not exactly, but he did everything in dismal silence. I often had the impression I was having an affair with a corpse."

"No caresses?"

"In the beginning some, but later he cooled off completely. He was one of those old-fashioned men who believe that the purpose of marriage is only to have children. Since we couldn't have children, sexual relations were superfluous."

"Was he perverse in some sense?" I asked.

The woman thought it over. "In a sense, yes—you'll soon hear."

"What happened?" I asked.

"The worst trauma of our lives began with a joke."

"Whose joke?" I asked.

"Mine, not his. He was not a joker. Once in a while he tried to talk to me about stocks. God shouldn't punish me, but this topic bored me stiff. Later on I thought that I should have listened to him and shown some interest in his business, but somehow I couldn't do it. The moment he began to talk about it I started to yawn. I hated his business. A man should have a profession, do something, leave the house, not sit day and night and wait for stocks to go up or down a few cents. The fact is, he didn't allow me to leave the house. He kept me prisoner. When I did go out to buy food I had to tell him in advance where I was going, what I was going to spend, and how long I'd be out of the house. I can't understand to this day how I could bear all this for six years. A war was going on, the Jews in Europe were destroyed, and I rationalized that my situation was still better than languishing in a concentration camp.

"One evening we were sitting together in our living room. I read the first pages of the newspaper, and he took out the business section. Suddenly he said, 'The oils are depressed.'

"I don't know why, but I said, 'So am I.'

"I'm not sure whether I said it to myself or to him. He looked at me, astonished, sad, angry, and asked, 'Why are you depressed? What do you miss? You aren't happy with me?'

" 'It's only a joke,' I said.

" 'Do you regret that you married me?' he asked. 'Do you want a divorce?'

" 'No, Boris, I don't want a divorce,' I said.

" 'Am I not the right husband for you?' he continued. 'Am I too old for you?'

" 'And what if you are too old?' I asked. 'Can you become younger? Do you want to go to Professor Voronoff and implant monkey glands into your body?' I expected him to smile. I had heard there was a professor in Europe, I think in Switzerland, who tried to make the old young. I'm not sure Professor Voronoff was still alive at the time. I said it just to hear my own voice, perhaps to hear his voice. He looked at me not only with scorn but also with a kind of regret and pity. He said, 'I couldn't let you adopt a child, but if you want to adopt a young lover I have nothing against it.'

" 'Boris, I don't want to adopt anybody,' I said. 'It was just talk. It's time you weren't so literal, so serious.'

" 'Well, let it be so,' he said, and he left for the room he called his office.

"I think it was the winter of 1944. Hitler was on his way down, but the Jewish misfortune had no end. Reports came that all the Jews in Europe were doomed.

I never heard Boris say anything about the Jewish situation. I lived all those years with a man I never understood and who remained a stranger to me.

"A few weeks passed, I don't remember how many. The last few days Boris had left the house before breakfast and did not return for lunch, as was his custom. This was something new in our lives. One evening he came home late. I waited for him in the living room and was reading a book I had borrowed from the public library. I had left his supper in the kitchen, but he told me he'd already eaten in a restaurant. He told me a son of his sister in London, a boy of fourteen, had come from England some time ago. His sister had feared that some misfortune would happen to him in the bombardments. The boy, whose name was Douglas, was a prodigy in mathematics and physics. He was accepted here in New York at a school for prodigies. Boris had consented that the boy should live with us. 'You never told me much about your sister,' I said. 'I had the impression you two were at odds.'

" 'It's true,' he said, 'that we always disagreed. I was still a little boy when she married, to a man who was good for nothing, a perfect idiot, but her son, thank God, takes after my family, the Kozlovs. You won't have to be alone anymore. I want to tell you something else,' he continued. 'I've rented an office for myself. My business is expanding. I'm drowning in paperwork. I've begun to invest in stocks for some German refugees, and Brooklyn is too far for them. My office is in Manhattan.'

"Boris never spoke for so long, especially about his

family. As a rule he only reproached me, and then he didn't speak but screamed.

"I said to him, 'Everything comes so suddenly.'

" 'Not so suddenly,' Boris said. 'I thought everything over very carefully.'

" 'Why didn't you ever mention to me that your nephew is in America?' I asked.

" 'I mention it now. He's an unusual boy. I took to him right away. He arrived here through Halifax, Nova Scotia. I'm sure you'll like him. He'll study in a special school for talented youngsters. Everything has already been arranged. Since my office is free now, it can be his room. I'll buy him a bed, but until then he can sleep on the sofa. You have every right to say no. I'm not going to force him on you.'

" 'Boris, you know very well I'll agree,' I said.

" 'He'll be here tomorrow morning,' Boris said, and went to his room.

"My first reaction when I heard the news was joy. I could not stand the loneliness anymore. God must have heard my prayers, I thought. But it soon became clear to me that Boris had contrived the whole plan in his conspiratorial manner. Men like Boris are bound by their nature to make plans way in advance and execute them precisely. They forget nothing. Even though he excoriated Stalin and called him a bloodthirsty Asian and a Genghis Khan of the twentieth century, I often thought Boris was a Stalin himself. We'll never know what people like these think. They always weave spiderwebs of vengeance. Did Boris bring this boy to tempt me and to be able later to sue me for infidelity? Was he connected with a lawyer? Was he involved with another woman with a lot of money or stocks? I could have easily saved him these sly tricks. If he had asked me for a divorce I would have given it to him without difficulty. I could still have gotten a job as a chambermaid or a saleswoman in a department store. During the war unemployment had ended. Nevertheless, I decided not to let myself be caught like an animal in a net. I intended to treat the boy from England with friendship but not to allow myself to fall into any entanglements.

"The next day Douglas came, and I'm ashamed to admit to you I fell in love with him at first sight. He was beautiful, slender, and tall for his age. Besides, he had a warmth that simply bewitched me. He called me 'Aunt,' but kissed me like a lover. He told me about his parents, and from his talk it became clear to me that his mother was a Boris in a skirt. She was a businesswoman through and through and had become rich from the war. She was separated from her husband, Douglas's father. The whole Kozlov family consisted of pedants and misanthropes, but Douglas seemed to take after his father, who came from a noble background. Douglas showed me his father's photograph. All my yearnings for a child and love, all my femininity and longings for motherhood awakened in me. I kept reminding Douglas that he was still a child, that I could have been his mother, but he refused to listen to me.

"A day or two after Douglas's arrival Boris began to go to the office every morning, and I knew it was not accidental. There were times I wanted to ask Boris,

'What's the meaning of all this? What are you aiming at?' But I knew he would not tell me the truth. Along with my love for the boy I was assaulted by a silent fear of cold and cunning calculations. Someone had prepared a trap for me, and I was destined to fall into it."

"Did you fall into it?" I asked.

The old woman hesitated for a while. "Yes."

"Immediately?" I asked.

"Almost immediately," she said.

"How?"

"One night Boris did not come home to sleep. He had told me he was going to Boston, but I knew it was a lie. What did I have to lose? When a man goes to such lengths, a woman has nothing to hope for. Boris did not come home, and Douglas without asking came into my bed. I never knew that a young boy like that could be so passionate."

"Those are supposed to be the man's strongest years," I said.

"Really? For me, it was partially curiosity and resignation. When someone spits on you you don't owe him any loyalty. Instead of spending one night in Boston, Boris was gone three nights. I knew for sure he was in New York. Boston is not a center of stock speculation. When he finally called us and said that he was back in New York, I told him, 'What you wanted happened.'"

"What did he say?" I asked.

"He said that he did it all for me. I said, 'You didn't have to bring your nephew from England. You didn't have to go into such acrobatics,' but he kept on saying that he had seen that I was unhappy and he wanted to help me. I was afraid that he might try to punish Douglas. Who knows what goes on in such a crippled brain? However, when he came home that evening he was as friendly to the boy as before. He asked him many questions about school. We ate supper together, and I was surprised to see that Douglas did not show any embarrassment. Could a boy of his age be so clever and cynical? Did the two of them have an agreement? I still don't know the answer."

"How long did the whole thing last?" I asked.

"He came in the summer, and in the fall he was accepted at a college, not here in New York but somewhere in the Middle West. He came to bid me farewell, and we spent the evening together. He told me that he would never forget me, that I'd enriched his life. He even promised he'd visit me on his winter vacation. He had never smoked before, but that evening he smoked one cigarette after another. He brought me flowers and a bottle of cognac. I put the flowers into a vase and poured myself a tea glass of the drink, which I gulped down in the bathroom. He asked me about his uncle, and I told him that he would come home late but that I had to go to sleep early and he must leave. 'Why, Auntie?' he asked, and I said, 'Because I'm tired.' 'I hoped that we would spend the night together,' he said, and I said, 'The last night one has to spend with oneself.'

"He kissed me, and I told him to leave. He hesitated for a while, and then he left. I waited for a minute or two and then I jumped out the window. We lived on the fourth floor. Thank God, I fell on the pavement and not on an innocent passerby."

"You had made the decision earlier?" I asked.

"No, but I knew all the time that this was what Boris expected and I had to comply."

"Still, you remained alive and he did not succeed," I said.

"Yes, to my regret. This is the whole story. I once heard you say on the radio that you take many of your themes from readers who come to tell you their stories, and I decided to be one of them. All I ask is that you change the names."

"What does a person think in such seconds?" I asked.

"In such seconds one doesn't think. One does what fate wants one to do."

"What has happened since then?"

"Nothing really. I broke my arms. I broke my legs. I broke my skull, and the doctors tried to mend me. They are still trying."

"Where's Boris?"

"I never heard from him or his nephew. I believe they both are somewhere in England."

"You're not divorced?"

"What for? No. I get reparation monies from the Germans. I need little, but every few weeks I must go to the hospital. Thank God, I'm not forced to become a public charge. I won't live too much longer. I came to tell you only one thing: that of all the hopes a human being can have, the most splendid is death. I tasted it, and whoever tasted this ecstasy must laugh at all the other so-called pleasures. That which man fears from the cradle to the grave is the highest joy."

"Still, seldom does anyone want to speed up this kind of joy," I said.

The woman did not answer and I thought she had not heard my words, but then she said, "The anticipation is part of the joy."

Translated by the author and Lester Goran

The Smuggler

THE TELEPHONE rang, and when I answered I heard a murmuring, a stuttering, and coughing. After a while a man said, "You most probably forgot about it, but you once promised to inscribe my books, I mean your books. In Philadelphia where we met you gave me your address and telephone number. Your address is the same but you've changed your telephone to a private number. I got it from your secretary, but I had to promise her that I wouldn't take much of your time."

He tried to remind me of my speech that evening in Philadelphia, and I realized it had happened some ten years ago. He said to me, "Are you hiding? In those days one could still find you in the telephone book. I do the same thing in my own small way. I avoid people."

"Why?" I asked.

"To explain this would take too much time and I promised not to bother you too long."

We made an appointment. He was supposed to come

to my apartment late in the evening. It was in December and a heavy snow had fallen in New York. From his idiomatic Yiddish it was clear to me he must be one of those Polish refugees who emigrated to the United States long after the war. Those who came to America in the earlier years interspersed their Yiddish with English words. I stood at the window and looked out on Broadway. The street below was white and the sky had a violet tinge. The radiator was seething quietly and sang out a tune which reminded me of our tiled stove on Krochmalna Street and the kerosene lamp over my father's desk. From experience I knew that those who make appointments with me come earlier than the agreed time. I expected any moment to hear a ringing at the door, but half an hour passed and he did not show up. I was looking for stars in the reddish sky, but I knew in advance that I would not find one in the New York heavens. Then I heard something like a scratch at my door. I went to open it and I saw a little man behind a pushcart piled high with books. In the cold winter my guest wore a shabby raincoat and a shirt with an open collar and a knitted cap on his head. He asked, "Your door has no bell?"

"Here's the bell button," I said.

"What? I'm half blind. It all comes with the years. We don't die at once but on the installment plan."

"Where did you get so many books of mine? Well, come in."

"I don't want to make your rug wet. I will leave the cart outside. No one will steal it."

"It doesn't matter. Come in."

I helped the man push the cart into the corridor. "I didn't know I'd brought out so many books," I said, and then I asked, "Have I really written so many books in my life?"

"They're not all yours. I also have books about you here, and various magazines and journals as well as translations."

After a while we went into the living room, and I said, "It's winter outside and you're dressed as if it were summer. Aren't you cold?"

"Cold, no. My father, he should rest in peace, used to say, 'No one wears a mask to cover one's nose. The nose doesn't get cold. A poor man is all made of nose flesh.'"

He smiled, and I saw that he had no teeth. I asked him to sit down. He looked to me like those men who live outdoors, like one of those beggars and bums one sees on the Bowery and in the hotels for the homeless. But I also saw the gentleness in his narrow face and in his eyes.

"Where do you keep all these books?" I asked. "In the apartment where you live?"

He shrugged his shoulders. "I live nowhere," he said. "In our little village in Poland there were yeshiva boys who ate every day in a different home. I sleep every night in a different house. I have a brother-in-law, the husband of my late sister, and I sleep in his house two nights a week. I have a friend, a landsman, and I can sleep over there when there's a need. I used to live in a building in Williamsburg in Brooklyn, but the house was condemned and they wrecked it. While I was sick in the hospital, thieves stole everything except my books. My landsman keeps them in his basement. I get reparation money from the Germans. After what happened to my family and my people I don't want to be settled any-place."

"What did you do before the war?" I asked.

The man pondered for a while and smiled. "I did what you told me to do in one of your articles, to smuggle myself, to sneak by, to muddle through. I was reading you in Poland. You once wrote that human nature is such that one cannot do anything in a straight line. You always have to maneuver between the powers of wickedness and madness.

"In the time of the First World War, I was still a little boy, but my mother and sister smuggled meat from Galicia and brought back from there tobacco and other contraband. Without this we all would have starved to death. When they were caught they were beaten cruelly. There were five children in our home, an old grandmother, a cripple, and my father, who could do nothing except study Mishnah and recite psalms or the Zohar. I asked him why all these plagues descended on us and he said the same thing you said. In exile one cannot live normally. One must always steal one's way among those who have the power and carry weapons. The moment a man gets some power he becomes wicked, my father said. The one who keeps a knife stabs, the one who has a gun shoots, and the one who has a pen writes laws which are always on the side of the thieves and murderers. When I became older and I began to read worldly books, I convinced myself that what my father said about the Jewish people was true about the whole human race, and even about the animals. The wolves devour the sheep, the lions kill the zebras. In later years we had in our village Communists who said that Comrades Lenin and Stalin would bring justice, but it soon became clear that they behaved like all the others who had power in all generations. Today a victim, tomorrow a tyrant. I read about Darwin and Malthus. These were the laws of life, and I decided my father was right. After Poland became independent smuggling ceased, but as always might was right. I hadn't learned any trade, and even if I'd learned how to be a tailor or a shoemaker I hadn't the slightest desire to sit ten hours a day and sew buttons or tack heels and soles on boots. I certainly did not have the desire to get married and create new victims for the new killers. Two of my younger brothers had become Communists and ended up in Stalin's prisons or the gold mines of the north. A third brother went to Israel and fell from an Arab bullet. My parents and a sister died because of the Nazis. Yes, I became a smuggler, and what I smuggled was myself. My body is my contraband. My coming here to America in 1949 was, I may say, a triumph of my smuggling. The chances for me to remain alive and come to the United States were smaller than small. If you ask me what my occupation is, my answer is, 'I am a Yiddish poet.' How can you know whether a person is a poet or not? If an editor needs to fill a hole in his magazine and he publishes a poem of yours, then you are a poet. If it doesn't happen, then you're just a graphomaniac. I never had any luck with editors and so I belong to the second category."

"May I ask why you need autographs?" I said.

"Some little madness everyone must have. If Jack the Ripper were resurrected from his grave, people would run to get his autograph, especially women. I was given an ego, a wanter, and I wage war with it. It wants to eat but I tell it to fast. It wants honors but I bring shame on it. Ego-shmego, I call it, hunger-shmunger. I do everything to spite it. It wants fresh rolls for breakfast and I give it stale bread. It likes strong coffee but I make it drink tepid water from the faucet. It still dreams about young women but it remains a virgin. Ten times a day I tell it, 'Get away from me, I need you like a hole in the head; you play the part of a friend but you're my worst enemy.' Just for spite I make it read old newspapers which I find on the floor of the subway. Thank God, I'm the stronger one, at least strong enough to make it miserable."

"Do you believe in God?" I asked.

"Yes, I do. The scientists tell us that a cosmic bomb exploded twenty billion years ago and created all the worlds. A week does not pass when they don't discover new parts in the atom and new functions. Just the same, they maintain that it's all an accident. They've gotten a new idol which they call evolution. They ascribe more miracles to that evolution than you can find in all the books about saints in all the religions. It's good for their rapacious business. Since there is no God, no plan, no purpose, you can hit and cheat and kill with a clean conscience."

"What is your God?" I asked. "A heavenly wolf?"

"Yes, a cosmic wolf, the dictator of all dictators. It

is all His work: the hungry wolf, the frightened sheep, the struggle for existence, the cancers, the heart attacks, insanity. He created them all, Hitler, Stalin, Chmielnicki, and Petlyura. It is said that He creates new angels every day. They flatter Him, sing odes to Him, and then they are liquidated, just like the old Bolsheviks."

He became quiet, and I inscribed the adult books, the children's books, and his magazines. "Where did you get all this?" I asked.

"I bought it, I didn't steal it," he said. "When I can save up a few dollars I buy books, not only yours; mostly scientific ones."

"But you don't believe in the scientists," I said.

"Not in their cosmology and sociology."

"If you'd like, you can leave me some of your manuscripts," I said. "I'd be glad to read your poems."

My guest hesitated for a while. "What for? It's not necessary."

"I feel that you have talent," I said. "Who knows? You may be a great poet."

"No, no, not by any measurement. A man has to be something and I dabble in poetry. Thank you for the good words, anyhow. Who needs poetry in our times? Not even the poets."

"There are some who need it."

"No."

My guest stretched out one hand to me and with the other began to push his wagon. I accompanied him to the door. I proposed to him again that I would like to read his works, and he said, "I thank you very much. What can poetry do? Nothing. There were quite a number of poets among the Nazis. In the day they dragged out children from their cribs and burned them, and at night they wrote poems. Believe me, these two actions don't contradict one another. Absolutely not. Good night."

Translated by the author and Lester Goran

A Peephole in the Gate

I WAS invited to South America by the Yiddish press. On the Argentinian boat I occupied a luxury cabin that had a Persian rug, soft chairs, a plush sofa, and a private bath, as well as a large window facing the water. The first-class passengers were outnumbered by the crew assigned to serve them. There was a special wine steward just for my table, and every time I took a sip from my glass he immediately refilled it. Luncheon and dinner meals were always accompanied by an eight-piece band. The bandleader was told that I was a Polish Jew living in America, and in my honor he often played Polish, Palestinian, and Yankee melodies. Almost all the other passengers were South Americans. In spite of all this catering I suffered from ennui. I could converse with no one and it is also difficult for me to strike up easy acquaintanceships with strangers. I had brought a chess set but couldn't find a partner, and one day I went to second class to look for one. There were only two classes.

The first class was half empty, while the second class hummed with activity. In the large lounge, men were drinking beer from mugs, others were playing cards, checkers, and dominoes. Women sat in groups and sang Spanish folk songs. Some of the faces seemed strangely wild, reminding me of animals or birds. I heard brutal voices. Women with enormous bosoms and behinds ate out of baskets and laughed with uncanny joy. A giant with mustaches that reached to his shoulders and brush-like brows told jokes in Spanish and his belly shook like bellows. The others applauded and stamped their feet. In the crowd I recognized a passenger from first class whom I had been seeing in the dining room three times a day. He sat there by himself. He always wore a tie and jacket, even for breakfast. Here he walked around in an open shirt, exposing a gray-haired chest. His face was red and he had white brows and a veined nose. I thought he was a Latin, but now, to my amazement, I saw him carrying a New York Yiddish newspaper. Approaching him, I said, "In that case let me say *sholem aleichem* to you."

His brown eyes, which had bluish bags under them, looked at me in astonishment for a while, and then he replied, "Is that so? *Aleichem sholem.*"

"What are you trying to find in second class?" I asked him.

"What are you doing here? Come, let's go out on the deck."

We went outside and sat down on two steamer chairs.

The ship was approaching the equator and the weather was warm. Sailors, stripped to the waist, sat on coils of mooring rope and played with greasy cards. One sailor was painting a beam while another was sweeping up the rubbish on the deck with a long broom. The air stank of vomit and fish. I said, "The crowd here is having a much better time than we upstairs."

"Sure, that's the reason I come down here. Do you live in New York?"

"Yes, in New York."

"I lived in New York for years, but then I moved to Los Angeles. I was told it was a paradise, but the winters are cold and we have smog in addition."

"I see that you were not born in America."

"I am from Warsaw. Where are you from?"

"Also from there."

"We lived at Grzybowska, number 5."

"I went to cheder at Grzybowska, number 5," I remarked.

"At Moshe Yitzhak's?"

The moment the man mentioned this name, he became like a relative to me. The distance of the ocean and the whole foreign atmosphere vanished in one second. He told me that at home he was Shlomo Mair, but in America his name was Sam. He had left Poland over fifty years ago. "How old do you think I am?" he asked.

"I would say in the sixties."

"I will be seventy-five in November."

"You are well preserved."

"Well, I had a grandfather who lived to the age of a

hundred and one. In America if you don't get a heart attack or cancer you keep on living. In the old country people died from typhoid fever or perhaps even from hunger. My father rented out flat-bottomed wagons to merchants. We had horses and stables and employed over a dozen coachmen. We lived in comfort. My father sent me to cheder and also hired a private tutor for me. I studied a little Russian, a little Polish, and what have you. My mother came from a better house. Her father was a lawyer—not a lawyer like here. He didn't attend a university. He filed petitions, sometimes served as an arbiter, and held the litigant's money in escrow. My mother wanted to make a scholar out of me, but I was not cut out for an education. My brother, Benjamin, and I had a pigeon coop on our roof and we used to stand there for hours chasing the pigeons with long sticks. We also went out with girls and attended the Yiddish theater on Muranow Place as well as the Polish one—Nowy, Letni, the opera. On Leszno Street there was a summer theater called the Alhambra, and there it was easy to pick up a serving girl. All the maids got half a day off on Sundays, and for a bar of chocolate a girl gave you everything. In those days men were not careful. The girl got pregnant and her mistress threw her out. There was a special clinic for such cases where each unwed mother had to nurse her own baby for six months as well as several foundlings. These children usually grew up and became firemen, janitors, and sometimes policemen. What became of the girl babies I really don't know. Respectable women at that time hired wet nurses, and these illegitimate mothers made a living that way. There were men whose business it was to impregnate these women, and for that they got a bowl of soup or a slice of bread. Since you are from Warsaw you should know these things yourself."

"I know, I know."

"Well, I had my share of the fun. I always had a pocketful of money and with a gulden it wasn't difficult to come by. If we wanted to, we went to the brothels in Poczajow and Tamka. Do you care to listen to more?"

"Yes I do."

"Since you're from Warsaw, too, why don't we share a table?"

"I would be happy to sit with you."

"I will speak to the dining-room steward. Sitting alone becomes lonely and one doesn't know what to do with oneself. So I eat a lot and gain weight. The Latins can eat without end. Did you notice their females? How can one get close to such a mountain of flesh? In the States, everybody is on a diet. Here they stuff themselves like gluttons. Do you drink beer?"

"No."

"Then I will order some for myself."

"As long as you are young," Sam continued, "you don't look into things too deeply, but when you get older you want someone to love who loves you. To pay for it is no trick. I became acquainted with a girl from Gnoyna Street. Her name was Eve—just like the Eve who gave Adam the forbidden apple and because of this all men must die. She seemed like a decent girl, with a round face, shapely legs, and a nice body. Eve was eighteen and years ago this wasn't so young anymore.

My mother didn't approve of the match, because her father was poor. He worked in the kosher slaughter-house, where his job was to skin the animals. Eve came from a large family and didn't have any dowry. But what did I need a dowry for? I knew I could make a living. An engagement party was arranged and plates were broken for good luck. I wasn't exceptionally pious so I took her to the theater on the Sabbath. During the week we used to go to a delicatessen where we ate hot frankfurters on rolls with mustard and washed them down with beer. Such crispy rolls as they baked in Warsaw are not to be gotten anywhere else; they melted in your mouth. Well, it was a real love affair. Fifty years ago an engaged couple did not behave as they do today. A girl had to remain a virgin until her wedding, but we did plenty nevertheless. This gave us a glimpse into the pleasures we would give each other after the wedding. We were already arguing about how many children we would have. I wanted six and she ten. Her father set the date for the Friday after Tisha b'Av, though this seemed like an eternity to me. It wasn't easy for a poor man to marry off a daughter, especially without a dowry. My parents gave Eve fine gifts: a gold watch, a chain, a brooch. Her father could not afford to give me any-thing of much value. He bought me a silver goblet for the Sabbath benediction over the wine. It was all a game to us and our love burned like fire.

"I will tell you what happened. Even talking about it now makes my blood boil. It was Saturday and we attended the theater. I still remember that they played *Chasha the Orphan*. After the play we went to Kotik's restaurant and had a big supper: fish, meat, and all the trimmings. Her father had an eleven o'clock deadline for her to be home. If she came in late he took the belt off his pants and whipped her like a small girl. I approved of his strictness. I didn't want to marry a run-around. As a matter of fact, when we became engaged, I stopped chasing the shiksas. Eve made it very plain that what I had done before was past, but now I was hers. It wasn't always easy to keep my promise. We had a maid and I used to go to her at night in the kitchen, but I had given Eve my word that I would behave. That Saturday night after we finished our meal we took a droshky from Nalewki Street to her home. It was not long after Passover. They used to close the gates in Warsaw about ten-thirty and when we got there the gate was already closed. We kissed before the gate, again and again, and then I rang the bell. The janitor's son came to open it. His name was Bolek—a mean fellow, a bully. He was often followed by a vicious dog.

"Most of the gates in Warsaw had a small peephole for the janitor to look through when someone rang the bell, because it might have been a burglar or a prowler. As a rule, when I took Eve home, it didn't occur to me to look through the peephole. What was there to see? This time I yearned for her so much that I wanted to watch her walk from the gate into the courtyard. I bent down and I almost died from shock. If there was an open grave before me I would have jumped into it. Eve was standing there kissing and hugging Bolek. I thought that I was seeing things or that I had lost my mind. They kept embracing and kissing like old lovers. This lasted for about ten minutes. I was stronger than iron or I would have had apoplexy on the spot. I won't burden you with what I went through that night. I tossed in bed as if I had a high fever. I wanted to hang myself. My mother came into my room and said, 'Shloimele, what's the matter with you?' I could not tell her about my disgrace, so I gave her some excuse. I suffered the most terrible torments until daybreak. In the morning I fell asleep, and when I awoke my mouth felt as bitter as gall. I decided that I could no longer remain in Warsaw. Many people from my neighborhood had gone to America. All one needed was passage. There were agents who got you a ticket for the ship and allowed you to pay it out in installments after finding work in America. My father had a strongbox where he kept his money. I knew where the key was hidden. When my father left for the stables and my mother went to Ulrich's Bazaar to do her shopping, I opened the strongbox and took two hundred rubles. There were many thousands there, but I wasn't a thief. I sent the first monies I earned in America back home, but this is already putting the cart before the horse.

"I went to Gnoyna Street, where Eve lived, and I walked up the stairs. Usually I went there Saturdays and Wednesdays. I found Eve standing in the kitchen frying a pancake. No one else was at home. She saw me and her face lit up. 'Shloimele,' she exclaimed, and tried to kiss me. I said, 'Don't let the pancake burn.' 'What brought you so early in the morning?' and I said, 'Someone told me that the jeweler we bought your gifts from is a swindler. The gold is not pure fourteen-karat. It's mixed with silver.' She seemed frightened, and taking the pan from the stove, she went to bring me the jewelry. I put it all into my pocket and caught her by the hair. She became pale as death. 'What are you doing?' she asked. 'I watched you through the peephole last night and saw what you did with Bolek.' She lost her tongue. I gave her one swift punch in the mouth and she began to spit out her teeth. She spat out one tooth and then a second and then a third. The best dentist couldn't have done a better job. I felt like killing her, but I am not a killer. I spat at her and left.

"My dear man, what is your name? Isaac? My dear Isaac, I didn't take leave of my father or my mother or of my brother, Benjamin—no one. I ran to the Vienna station and bought a ticket for Mlawa. I knew that there one could cross the border illegally into Prussia. The contrabandists—they were called guides—smuggled you over the border with a passport for three rubles. I had nothing with me. Not even a shirt. The guide asked me, 'Where's your bundle?' 'My bundle is here,' I said, and pointed to my heart. He understood what I meant. At night I crossed the border and early in the morning I took a train to Hamburg, where I bought a ticket for the ship to New York. I still had a nice sum left from the two hundred rubles. I also sold Eve's presents and bought myself ready-made linen, a suit, and a pair of German shoes.

"I traveled steerage, and even though I considered myself a modern man, I refused to eat non-kosher food. The truth is, I could not eat at all. Most of the passengers suffered from seasickness and vomited their guts out. You could have died from the stench. I was also sick, but it was in my head. I was afraid I would lose my mind. I now hated all women. Lifting my hands to heaven, I swore never to marry."

"Did you keep your word?"

"I have six grandchildren."

Sam asked, "Shall I continue? You want to hear more?"

"Please do."

"It's a long story but I won't drag it out. Can the story of a person's lifetime be told? In the Yiddish papers they print stories that go on for months or even for years. I read them. I love to read. To me, a writer is greater than a rabbi or a doctor. He knows everything that goes on in your soul as though he were right there. But when I travel I cannot get the papers. Someone in America saves them for me and when I come home I read the entire batch of them. Yes, I swore never to marry, but to be alone is also difficult. Years ago those who went on a ship to America became like one big family. We called ourselves ship brothers and ship sisters. Since we refused to eat non-kosher food, all we got was potatoes in their jackets and the brine of herring. In Hamburg I had spent some of the money I had with me to buy kosher salami and liverwurst, and on the ship I treated everyone. This made me a real king. The girls and women all came to me for a slice of wurst and they praised me and kissed me, but I knew it was all for the wurst. After what happened with

Eve I trusted no one. Among us greenhorns there was
a little young woman who was returning to America.
She had gone back to Europe to bring over her aunt.
They both occupied a cabin, but the old woman became
seasick, so the niece spent most of her time with us, the
immigrants. Her husband was a ritual slaughterer in
Brownsville. What did we know about Brownsville?
In Warsaw the wife of a ritual slaughterer wore a wig
or a bonnet, but this woman went about with her head
uncovered. She was dark, with laughing eyes. She
pulled jokes out of her sleeve. Every day I gave her a
large slice of salami. She nicknamed me Baby, even
though I was tall and she so tiny I could have put her in
my pocket. She was a big talker and clever as the
dickens. For her, things didn't have to be spelled out.
One look and she knew all about you, like a gypsy. Her
name was Becky. Though her real name was Breindel,
in America it became Becky. I never met anyone so
quick. She was everywhere and knew everything. She
hopped around like a bird. Of course she could speak
English. She said to me, 'Baby dear, if one woman was
false to you, it isn't necessary to blame all of us.' 'How
do you know that a woman was false to me?' I asked.
'Baby, it's written on your forehead,' she answered. The
next day Becky invited me to her cabin. Her aunt lay
there as if she were dead. Seasickness is a terrible thing.
I thought that she was dying, but Becky was laughing
and winking at me. She signaled me to lean toward her
while she raised herself on her tiptoes. She gave me a
kiss that I still remember. That the wife of a ritual
slaughterer should kiss a strange man was something

new to me. I said to her, 'Don't you love your husband?' and she replied, 'Yes, I do love him, but he's busy slaughtering in Brownsville and I'm here.' 'If he knew what you were doing he would slaughter you, too.' And she said, 'If people knew the truth, the world would collapse like a house of cards.' We made love right then and there. I never knew that such a small woman could have such large desires. She tired me out, not I her. All the while she kept on prattling about God. Sabbath Eve she put three candles into three potatoes, draped a shawl over her head, covered her eyes with her fingers, and blessed the candles. And so we arrived in America. On the dock a large crowd stood waiting for the new arrivals, and my piece of merchandise recognized her husband, the slaughterer. 'Listen, Baby,' she said to me, 'nothing happened between us. We are complete strangers, forget the whole thing.' I later saw her hugging the slaughterer. She kissed him and wept, and I renewed my oath never to believe a woman. Shloimele, I said to myself, it's a false world. Years later a rabbi told me that it's written in the Torah that all humans are liars."

"Not in the Torah," I said, "but in the Book of Psalms: 'I said in my haste, all men are liars.'"

"That's it. Most of the passengers were taken to Ellis Island. I was as healthy as a bear and had money, so they let me through immediately. Agents from all sorts of factories came to the ships, and the moment an immigrant landed they hired him to work. The pay was never more than three dollars a week and sometimes even less. Since I had money in my purse, I was not in a hurry to become a slave. Downtown there was a square called the Pig Market. People came there to look for work. Every tradesman carried his tools as a sign of his skill. I saw a tailor carrying the head of a sewing machine, a carpenter held a saw. This is how it is in America. In one trade there's a need for workers and in another it is slack. Everything depends on the season. Agents tried to employ me but I wanted to look around first. A young man came over and said, 'You cannot sleep in the street. Let's go and find lodgings for you.' We walked as far as Attorney Street. The streets were crowded. People ate in the street, read the papers in the street, discussed politics. Even though it was the middle of the day, a whore tried to lead us to her basement room for the price of a quarter, but we refused to go with her. It seemed that my companion was a middleman. He took me into an apartment on the third floor where boarders were lodged and introduced me to the missus. Her name was Molly. Molly is an Irish name, but it's also a Jewish name. The flat had only cold water and a toilet in the hall. If you wanted to take a bath you had to go to the barber. For two dollars a week, the landlady gave me bed and board—all three boarders in one room. Her husband was a house painter. She washed our linen for a few pennies extra. She was a decent woman who killed herself for her husband and her children, but her husband was a bum who ran around with others. Her daughter came home at two o'clock every night and necked with the boys right in front of the door. This Molly's cooking was fit for a king. How she could have given us all this for two dollars a week

I still don't understand. She bought bargains from the pushcarts on Orchard Street.

"My dear man. I held out and did not marry for ten years. I'm not a philosopher, but I kept my eyes open. I thought about life and saw what went on. As long as people believed in God they were afraid of the fires in Gehenna. But our Yiddish papers wrote that there was no God and that Moses was a capitalist and a bluffer. So what was there to fear?

"When I came to America there were already cars and even a few trucks, but most of the merchandise was carried in wagons. There were troughs on many of the streets with water for the horses. I knew all about horses from Warsaw and I went into the express business. At first I drove a wagon for another man, then I bought my own express wagon and a pair of Belgian mares. I soon bought a second wagon, and the number kept growing. I had entered America with my right foot and was lucky in whatever I did. I worked sixteen hours a day but I had more than enough strength. Today I take sleeping pills. At that time I would lie down on the bare floor in my wagon, and before I knew it, I was asleep. I could sleep without interruption for ten hours. Bums used to steal into my wagon and they slept there, too. Business was good and I became rich, or what was then thought of as rich. A thousand dollars bought more than ten thousand today. I had my own apartment on Grand Street. This was considered uptown. Matchmakers were after me, but I spoke to them openly: 'Why should I marry and let another man sleep with my wife? Let the

other one marry and I will sleep with his wife.' These
were not just words. Do you understand me?"

"Yes, I understand."

"No, you can't be too smart. Heaven and earth have
sworn that people cannot outwit fate. I already told you
that I love the Yiddish theater. Can you latecomers
know what the Yiddish theater meant to us? The great
actors were still alive then: Adler, Tomashefsky,
Madame Liptzin, and later Kessler. Most of the shop-
workers could go to the theater only on Saturdays, but
I, a bachelor with money, could go whenever the desire
came to me—and it came to me almost every night.
Today's plays are worthless. In the Yiddish plays I'm
talking about there was something to see—King David,
Bathsheba, the Destruction of the Temple—real history!
The Jews fought the Romans and the whole battle was
right before your eyes. I had plenty of women and girls
to take out, but I often liked to go to the theater by myself. There was one actress, Ethel Sirota, whose name
was printed in small letters, but the first time I saw her
act it made my heart jump. She hasn't been onstage now
for God knows how many years. She is the grandmother
of my grandchildren.

"If I were to tell you how I became acquainted with
her and how I took her away from her husband, I'd
have to sit with you three days and three nights. How
did I, a simple coachman from Warsaw, come to an
American actress? But love has strange power. She
later admitted to me that she often felt my gaze on her
all during the show. I always bought a ticket for the

first or second row. Her husband acted in the road companies. He was never engaged for the New York productions. I once saw him act in Philadelphia—a piece of wood. They had no children. Well, we fell in love. The first time I went out with her I thought I would go mad with happiness. We ate in a restaurant on Broadway and afterward went to a nightclub. There were plenty of naked women in the show but I was burning with passion for Ethel. We drank champagne and I became tipsy. 'What do you see in me?' she asked. 'My husband is ready to trade me in for the lowest yenta.' And I told her that what I saw in her could not be put into words. We kissed and each kiss was like fire. Just as they write in the novels. The very first night I proposed marriage to her. When her husband, that lughead, heard that someone else was interested in his wife, he again developed an appetite for her and a game of cat and mouse began. He finally convinced himself that it was me she wanted, not him, and he demanded money. I counted out two thousand dollars in cash. Then it was a fortune—and he divorced her. It's easier said than done. It didn't happen quite that fast. Actually it dragged out for a long time and while waiting we lived as man and wife.

"When we became close and I began to question her about her past, she swore to me that her husband was the only man she ever had. But I will give you a rule: If a woman tells you that you are her second, you can be sure you are her tenth, twentieth, or perhaps her fiftieth. It's written someplace in the Bible that snakes creeping on rocks and ships crossing the sea leave no trace.

If I'm not mistaken, King Solomon said it, and you know what he was referring to. The more I queried her, the more I learned. Before she appeared in the New York theaters, she, too, acted in the road companies, and in order to get a part you had to sleep with the director or whoever was in charge. Actually it wasn't much different on Second Avenue. Without liquor Ethel kept silent, but the moment she got high she spoke freely. I jotted down a long list of her lovers, and each time I thought the list was complete, another name popped up. Meanwhile she became pregnant. I had taken her from her husband and because of me she had left the theater—how could I destroy her life? We quarreled and it came to blows. Her tears could have moved a stone. I realized that this was my fate. Eve kissed the janitor's son and Ethel sold herself for a part. Now that she was married and pregnant, she promised to behave. But she could not give up the theater altogether. We went to see all the shows. She got the tickets for nothing. Every cashier knew her. Once you have been part of the Yiddish theater, you are never forgotten. Ethel gave birth to a girl and we called her Fanny, or Feigele, after Ethel's mother. Two years later she had twins, a boy and a girl. These are my children.

"After her second delivery she again yearned for the theater. Parts were offered to her, the telephone kept ringing, but I told her in no uncertain terms that if she returned to the stage I would leave her. Before marriage I looked upon actors as gods, but when I learned how they conducted themselves and how the girls had to sleep around to get parts, I stopped worshipping them. On the stage you see a man dressed like a rabbi in a satin coat and a fur hat, reciting 'Hear, O Israel,' and sacrificing himself for the Holy Name. Two hours later he would be telling some aspiring wench either to go to bed with him or forget about the theater. I had good friends and the minute they came to my house they started to warm up to my wife. She was pleased. Why not? But after what happened to me in Warsaw at Eve's gate I lost my taste for such monkey business. When one of my cronies got too close to Ethel, I grabbed him by the collar and showed him the way out. This gave me the reputation of being a jealous savage. Ethel lamented that I was driving our friends away. I stopped going to the Yiddish theater and the English one didn't attract me. There they don't act, they just recite.

"In time the express wagons were all replaced by trucks, so I formed a trucking company. Everything would have been all right, but my blood was poisoned already. When I wasn't brooding about Ethel, my thoughts returned to the double-dealing of the slaughterer's wife. At night when I lay with Ethel I questioned her about all her lovers. She had to confess every single detail. If she denied anything I gave her hell. In every type of business one has to travel occasionally, but each time I imagined that the minute I left town, Ethel's lover would be with her. I was successful with women and when I saw how other women behaved I felt that Ethel could not be different. Just as soon as you turn your back your wife is already winking at someone else. It's like a grabbag game. Things reached such a state that I had to go to a nerve doctor. Instead of giving me a prescription he made things worse. He himself was divorced from his wife and he was paying her alimony. He pointed to his sofa and said, 'If this sofa could talk, many couples would be divorced.' At night I was tormented by bad dreams and they all had to do with my suspicious nature. I would awaken in the middle of the night with an urge to strangle Ethel. I couldn't have done it, but I was overcome with rage. And when I realized that two daughters were growing up in my own house and that they would one day be as sly as the other females, I wanted to kill them, too—my own children. Do you understand such insanity? Do you consider me a murderer?"

"You are not a murderer."

"What am I?"

"A man."

They rang the gong for supper and we both went up to the first-class dining room. Sam arranged with the steward to seat us at the same table. My wine steward now served both of us. Between one course and the next there was a long wait, because every dish was cooked to order. The supper lasted two hours.

I asked Sam, "Did you stay with Ethel?"

He pushed his plate aside.

"We were divorced. I wanted to leave New York and she wouldn't live away from it. She kept on dragging me to the Yiddish theater and the Café Royale, where she met her former boyfriends. As soon as I sat down at the table with my wife we were immediately joined by some rascal who had slept with her. I could not put up with it. I may be a simple fellow, the son of a coachman, but in our home such goings-on did not exist. My mother, peace be with her, had one God and one husband. I was so overwrought I was close to killing Ethel and then committing suicide, because I was not cut out to rot in prison or go to the electric chair. Our fighting and quarreling continued for so long it turned our love sour. She became, what do you call it, frigid. She complained that when I made love to her it was painful. I went with her to the nerve doctor and he said, 'It's in her head.' We parted, then made peace, then parted again. When Ethel finally did go back to the theater, the play folded the first week. The editor, I've forgotten his name, wrote that the whole performance was one long yawn. He didn't even mention Ethel's name. These critics pay attention only to the big shots. Now it was she who demanded the divorce. I haven't fallen so low that I would force myself on anyone, so I sent her to Reno and all was finished. Of course I supported the children. She believed that once she got rid of me all the theaters would be open for her, but they kept on closing, one after another. The new generation does not know Yiddish. And why go to a theater downtown, when for forty cents you can see in your own neighborhood a Hollywood movie with music, dancing, and gorgeous girls. She lived without a man for six years and refused to speak to me when I came to see the children. She locked herself in the bedroom or left the house. Later she married a druggist, a widower with five children. New York oppressed me. She poisoned the children against their father. My older daughter, Fanny, spat at me. Today she's a doctor. The younger one was married to an actor and tried to follow in her mother's footsteps, but it didn't work out and she was divorced. As a matter of fact, she's twice divorced. I don't even know where she is. I think somewhere in the Middle West. She studied nursing. My son is a scholar, a professor in Madison, Wisconsin. Sociology. He married a Gentile girl. This boy loved me. He used to visit me in Los Angeles. He has five beautiful children, but they are not Jews. Their mother sent them to Catholic parochial school. Sundays they had to go to church. Torn away from their roots!

"I moved to Los Angeles, first because I began to suffer from colds, second because I couldn't be in the same city as Ethel. Then I had a partner in business and partners are a heartache. Either they are lazy or they are thieves, and sometimes they are both. The Hitler war began and I read in the papers what they were doing to the Jews. My parents had long since died. My father, may he rest in peace, refused to come to America because here Jews worked on the Sabbath. My brother, Benjamin, fell in the First World War. My whole family was wiped out by the Nazis. I am far from being learned, but when I read how strong, healthy murderers dragged little children out of their cribs and later played ball with their skulls, I became desperate. While still in New York I used to go to the meetings of the *landsleit* or sometimes to a protest meeting at Madison Square Garden. What the speakers said made sense. They asked for money and I contributed. Just the same, I noticed that the people took it all lightly. I could see that even the speakers themselves didn't take it too much to heart. I was told that the speakers had to be paid and they even bargained about their fee. For some reason I took it to heart more than the others. Perhaps because I lived alone and had difficulty sleeping at night. I lay awake in my bed with the newspaper, and my brain whirred like a machine. If educated people could commit such cruelties while the rest of the world played dumb, what difference is there between a man and a beast? When you live with your family you don't have time to think. A wife lies near you, you are surrounded by children. When you are alone with the four walls you begin to take score. Well, I left for California.

"How could California help me? However, I began a new business and became very busy. In Santa Barbara I became acquainted with a widow, and it looked like love. As we kissed and caressed and fondled each other, I kept thinking in my heart that she had just put her husband, the father of her children, in his grave and now she was already replacing him. All my thoughts led in one direction: there is no love, there is no loyalty. Those with whom you are close will betray you even faster than total strangers. In the beginning the widow said that she demanded nothing from me, only that I should be friendly to her. Before I turned around I was supporting her. One day she wanted a mink coat and the next day a brooch or a diamond ring. Then she insisted that I take out a quarter of a million dollars' worth of insurance, not a penny less. I told her right off that if I had to pay, I would pay those younger and more beautiful. She raised a rumpus and I sent her away. She was too clever for her own good.

"Since then I have lived alone. From time to time little affairs begin, but as soon as I make it clear to them that I don't like to mix love with money, they run as if from a fire. I gave much thought to these matters. It is true that my mother was also supported, but she gave my father children, worked in the house from morning till late at night, and was a faithful wife. When my father had to go to Zichlin or to Wengrow, he didn't have to worry that some dandy would enter his home and kiss his wife. He could have gone to America for six years and my mother would have remained loyal to him. Modern women——"

"Your father was a faithful husband," I interrupted him. "But you demand faithfulness only from others."

He pondered and looked at me inquisitively.

"Yes, this is true."

"Your Eve kissed the janitor's son and you kissed the maid in your home."

"What? I promised Eve to be true, but from time to time I had to have a female, if not——"

"Without religion there is no faithfulness."

"So what shall I do? Pray to a God who let six million Jews be killed? I don't believe in God."

"If you don't believe in God you have to live with whores."

He didn't answer for some time, and then he said,

"Therefore I went away from everybody and everything."

Sam emptied his glass and the wine steward filled it at once. I also took a sip from my glass and this, too, was immediately replaced.

I asked, "Where are you running to—Buenos Aires?"

Sam pushed away his glass.

"I have nothing to do in Buenos Aires. I have nothing to do in any other country. I'm retired and have enough to live on even if I reach one hundred. I don't wish it on myself. What for? For a man like me, life is a curse. I had hoped that old age would bring me peace. I reckoned that after seventy a person stops musing about all petty things. But the head does not know how old it is. It remains young and full of the same foolishness as at twenty. I know that Eve is no longer alive. She must have perished in the Nazi slaughter. Even if she were alive she would be a tottering old woman by now. But in my mind she is still a young girl and Bolek, the janitor's son, is still a young boy and the gate is still a gate. I lie awake at night, not able to sleep a wink, and I burn up with rage at Eve. Sometimes I regret that I didn't hit her harder. I know that I would have married her if I hadn't looked through the peephole that night. Her father wanted to arrange the wedding in a hall. A carriage would have been sent for her, and Bolek would have been standing there winking and laughing."

"It may be," I said, "that if you didn't look through

the peephole that evening you would never have gone
to America. You and Eve and your children would all
have been burned in Auschwitz or tortured to death in
some other concentration camp."

"Yes, I thought about that, too. One look through a
peephole and your whole life is changed. You would
still have been here at this table, but not with me. Ethel
wouldn't have married the druggist. She would have remained the wife of that bully. She would never have
had any children. He was supposed to have been sterile.
That's what the doctors told her. What does all this
mean? That everything is nothing but a miserable accident."

"Perhaps God wanted you to live and therefore he
made you look into the peephole."

"Now, my dear man, you talk nonsense. Why should
God want me to live while millions of other people are
destroyed? There is no God. There isn't any. I have
no education, but I have brains in my skull, not straw.
I want you to know that I have a woman on this ship."
Sam suddenly changed his tone.

"In second class?"

"Yes, in second class. I told her that I am a shoemaker and that I am going to Buenos Aires because it's
cheaper there and I can live on my social-security pay-
ments."

"Who is she?"

"An Italian woman. She lives in Chile. She's returning from a visit to her sister in America, where she
stayed for three years and learned a little English. Four

of her six children are already married. I walked around on the deck and then I sat down near her steamer chair. We began to talk. She must have been pretty in her young days. Now she's over fifty and in those countries women age faster. I asked her questions and she told me everything. Her husband is Spanish and he's a barber in Valparaiso. Her sister in New York asked her to come because she had cancer. They live on Staten Island and are not poor people. When her sister's left breast was removed the doctors promised her that everything would be all right, but later she got it in the other breast. So my woman stayed with her until she died. The people from Chile don't know what lying is. They tell you everything provided you are a stranger. She told me the whole story of her life. Before she married and after, she had men. Her husband stood in the barbershop all day long, shaving and cutting hair, while she remained at home. One day it was a neighbor, the mailman, a boy from the grocery. They all asked for it and she seldom refused. The day she arrived in America her brother-in-law immediately began to bother her. He's an electrician. Since his wife was sick he did it with her. I said to her, 'Would you do it with me?' And she answered, 'Where? I share my cabin with three other women and two of them suffer from seasickness.' I told her that I could hire an empty first-class cabin. When she heard the words 'first class,' she got frightened. I persuaded her just the same. She made herself beautiful and I took her to my cabin. You speak about God. She's very pious. In Chile she went to church every Sunday. Even on Staten Island she didn't miss church. She never eats meat on Friday, only fish. But one thing has nothing to do with the other."

"Our mothers and grandmothers did not behave this way," I said.

"How do you know?"

"You yourself said that your father could rely on your mother."

"This is what I think. One can never be sure. If I had married Eve and we had children, they wouldn't have believed that their mother fooled around with the janitor's son."

"She might have been a very faithful wife."

"It may be. But during all the years she could never have forgotten what she had done. It may even be that Bolek would have visited her in our home a few months after our wedding and threatened to divulge her secret if she didn't give herself to him. You never know what such hoodlums are capable of doing when they are in heat."

"I know very well."

"I chattered so much about myself but I never asked you what you do. By the way, what street did you live on in Warsaw?"

"On Krochmalna Street."

"That was a street of thieves."

"I'm not a thief."

"What are you?"

"A Yiddish writer."

"Really? What is your name?"

I told him my name.

I expected him to jump with surprise, because I had

seen him read the newspaper to which I contribute. But he sat mute and looked at me with astonishment and sadness.

"Yes, it's you. Now that you mention it, I recognize you from the pictures. I've read every word you've ever written. I always dreamed of meeting you."

For minutes neither of us spoke. Then Sam said, "If this could happen to me on this ship, then there is a God."

Translated by the author and Ruth Schachmer Finkel

The Bitter Truth

THIS IS a story of two Warsaw youths—Zeinvel and Shmerl, both of them workers in a tailor shop. Shmerl was short, chubby, and had a round face and brown eyes which expressed naïveté and goodness. He was always nibbling on candy and cookies. He often smiled and burst out laughing for no reason at all.

Zeinvel was the complete opposite: tall, thin, with sunken cheeks and narrow shoulders. His disposition was often sour and gloomy. He seasoned every morsel of food with a lot of salt and pepper and washed it down with vodka.

As they say, opposites attract. Shmerl relished Zeinvel's sharp tongue, while Zeinvel found in Shmerl an attentive listener who looked up to him with wonder. Neither one was particularly learned, although Zeinvel knew a bit of the Pentateuch and Rashi, and could explain to Shmerl the articles and jokes printed in the Yiddish newspaper.

Needless to say, Zeinvel was more temperamental and more eager for the favors of the fair sex than Shmerl. But in those times it was difficult for a poor young man to find a woman, especially one of easy virtue. His only resort was to go every week to a brothel and for a gulden or twenty kopeks satisfy his needs. Shmerl always reproached Zeinvel for this light-minded conduct. First of all, he might catch a disease, and second, it went against Shmerl's grain to buy love; he would never enter such a loathsome place. Shmerl called himself a bashful shlemiel. Still, Zeinvel tried many times to persuade him to overcome his old-fashioned modesty and accompany him.

Finally, Shmerl gave in. To summon up the courage, he stopped off at a tavern and gulped down a mug of beer. When they arrived at the house and the door was opened, Shmerl recoiled and ran away. He had gotten a glimpse of heavily made-up women dressed in glaring colors: red, green, and blue stockings attached to lace garter belts. He inhaled an offensive odor and ran away with such speed that it was a miracle he didn't trip over his own steps. Later, when they met in the soup kitchen for dinner, Zeinvel scolded him.

"Why did you run away? Nobody would have chased you."

"Shameless women like these nauseate me. Don't be angry with me, Zeinvel, I have this sort of foolish nature and I almost vomited."

"*Nu*, they are lewd, but they don't bite. And we don't marry them. For the time being, let them be of some use . . . It's better than not sleeping at night."

"You're right, Zeinvel, but I have this silly nature . . ."

"*Nu*, I won't bother you anymore."

And that's how it remained. Zeinvel continued to go to the whorehouse every week. Shmerl admitted to Zeinvel that he often envied him, but he would never again try to seek pleasure from those wanton females. He would rather perish.

When the war between Russia and Germany broke out in 1914, the two friends were separated. Zeinvel was mobilized and Shmerl got a blue card of rejection because he failed to pass the physical examination. Zeinvel promised Shmerl to send a letter from the front, but soldiers are given few chances to write or to receive letters. Zeinvel lost all contact with Shmerl. He served in the Russian Army until Kerensky's revolution took place and then deserted. Only after the Polish-Bolshevik war did Zeinvel return to Warsaw and his tailor shop. Many young men Zeinvel knew in former years had died from typhoid fever. Others simply vanished— Shmerl among them. Zeinvel tried to come back to the old routine, but he had aged and was exhausted. He had witnessed so much betrayal and depravity that he no longer trusted any woman and had given up all hope of marriage. Yet the need for a woman cannot be denied, despite all disappointments. Zeinvel had no choice but to return to houses of ill repute. He made peace with the idea that this was his fate.

One day, as Zeinvel sat eating lunch in the old soup kitchen, he heard someone speaking his name. He turned around and recognized Shmerl, who had become as round as a barrel. He was dressed like a merchant and no longer had the appearance of a tailor's apprentice. The two friends fell on each other, kissed, embraced.

Shmerl cried out, "That I have lived to see this day means there is a God! I have searched for you for years. I thought you had already gone . . ." and he pointed his finger at heaven. "You don't look well," he went on. "You've become thinner than you were."

"And you've become wider than longer," Zeinvel said.

"Did you marry, by any chance?" Shmerl asked.

"Marry? No, I have remained a bachelor."

"*Nu,* that's why you look like this. Brother of mine, I have married and I'm happy," Shmerl said. "I don't live in Warsaw anymore, I moved to the town of Reivitz, and I'm not a tailor's apprentice. You may think I'm boasting, but I have found the best girl in all of Poland. There is no other wife like my Ruchele in the entire world. She is good, clever. She helps me in the store. What am I saying? She *is* the whole business. There are no children yet, but Ruchele is better than ten children. What are you doing, Zeinvel? Are you still going to those rotten whores on Smocza Street?"

"Do I have a choice?" Zeinvel said. "After all the wars and revolutions, there is barely a proper woman left in Warsaw. Nothing but used-up merchandise from King Sobieski's time."

"Really, I pity you, after having tasted a young and beautiful girl like my Ruchele, you just spit on this trash . . . *Oy,* this is a miracle! I would never have thought to enter this soup kitchen, but I was passing by and caught a whiff of borscht and fried onions.

Something drew me in. The whole meeting was absolutely destined!"

Shmerl did not leave Zeinvel's side until the next morning. He took a room for him in the guest house where he was staying, and they talked and prattled late into the night. Shmerl told Zeinvel how he had passed the war years in the provinces and met Ruchele there, and how it was love at first sight. He had been a worker long enough. From manual labor one cannot become rich. One toils a lifetime and one is left with nothing. He suggested to Zeinvel that he come to Reivitz and there he and his wife could find him a position and possibly a wife. He had told Ruchele everything about him. He had praised him so much that Ruchele became jealous. "Don't worry," Shmerl said. "Everything will be fine. She will be happy to meet you."

Zeinvel complained that his work had come to the point where it was suffocating him. He was sick and tired of the big city, the heavy scissors and irons being a burden to him, the constant grumbling of the customers. He could not find one single human being with whom he could be close. What could he make of himself here? He was prepared to travel with Shmerl to the end of the world.

Everything happened quickly. Zeinvel packed his few possessions in a valise and was ready for the trip.

They arrived in the town of Reivitz on Friday afternoon. Ruchele was working in the store, and a maid was preparing the Sabbath meal. Shmerl's house was clean, neat, and permeated with a spirit of rest which one often finds with a loving and happy couple. The maid welcomed Shmerl and his guest with a Sabbath cookie and plum pudding. Shmerl led Zeinvel to the washroom. Zeinvel dressed in his Sabbath clothing; he put on a fresh shirt and a tie, preparing to meet Shmerl's wife. He didn't need to wait long. The door opened and Ruchele came in. Zeinvel took one look at her and became as white as chalk. He knew her—she was one of the most sought-after harlots in the house he had frequented. She was known there as Rachelle. At the time, she was a young girl and was so much in demand that the men lined up for her favors. The other girls quarreled with her and constantly argued with the madame and the pimps. Rachelle was rare in the sense that she took pleasure in her debased profession. She spat fire and brimstone on so-called decent women. She laughed with insolence and with such gusto that her laughter shook the walls. She told stories she had heard in other bordellos and in prison. She was known among the guests as an insatiable whore, obsessed with men. So much so, that they had to throw her out of the brothel. Zeinvel had had her quite a number of times. Thank God, she did not recognize him. There was no doubt that this was Rachelle. She still had a scar on her cheek from being assaulted by a pimp some years ago. She had become a little more plump than before, and had grown more beautiful.

Zeinvel was so shocked that he lost his tongue altogether. He trembled and stuttered. His knees buckled and he saw sparks. He felt like running out the door, but he could not do that to Shmerl. He soon came to himself and greeted the woman as one greets the wife of a dear friend; she responded accordingly. There was not a trace of her former vulgarity. Even her city accent had changed. She carried herself like a woman born and raised in a decent home, friendly and tactful.

He heard her say, "Any friend of Shmerl's is a friend of mine."

That Friday night they all three ate the Sabbath meal. Although Zeinvel was careful not to ask any questions, she told him that she was an orphan on both sides and had worked a few years in a chocolate factory in Warsaw. It was clear to Zeinvel that she had chosen to put an end to her vile life. But how had this come about? Did some rabbi make her repent her sins? Did she suffer some terrible sickness which shattered her? Was it her love for Shmerl? Did she experience some startling event similar to what he was going through tonight? There was no point in racking his brains over an enigma which only God or perhaps death could solve. She was receiving Zeinvel with a dignity that had apparently become her second nature.

That night Zeinvel could not sleep. The two old friends had talked half the night. The rest of the night Zeinvel tossed and turned in his bed. The most wild thoughts assailed him: Should he wake up Shmerl and tell him the truth? Should he leave stealthily and run away in the direction of Warsaw? Should he tell Rachelle that he recognized her? He hoped that Shmerl was not the victim of treachery, like so many men he knew. Shmerl, the husband of the most salacious strumpet he had ever known! At this thought Zeinvel's body became alternately hot and cold and he heard his teeth chattering. Some perverse power made him play with the idea of taking advantage of Rachelle's dilemma for his own enjoyment. "No, I would rather die than commit an abomination like that," he murmured to himself. Dawn was breaking by the time he fell asleep.

Both man and wife greeted him in the morning: she with a glass of tea, and he with a Sabbath cookie, which one is allowed to take before the morning prayer.

"What is the matter with you? You look tired and pale," Shmerl said to him. "Did you have bad dreams?"

"Did my gefilte fish upset your stomach?" Rachelle asked playfully.

And he answered her, "I haven't eaten such delightful fish since I escaped from the Bolshevik paradise."

That morning, on the way to the synagogue, Zeinvel said, "Shmerl, I want to ask you something."

"What do you want to ask?"

"What is dearer to you? The truth or your comfort?"

"I don't know what you mean. Speak simple Yiddish," Shmerl said.

"Imagine that you were given a choice to know the truth and to suffer or to remain deceived and be happy, which would you choose?"

"You are speaking strangely. What do you mean?" Shmerl said.

"Answer me."

"What's the point of truth if people suffer from it? Why are you asking me all this?"

"There was an article about it in the Warsaw newspapers and they asked the readers to express their opinions," Zeinvel said.

"The newspapers print all kinds of nonsense. Someone may tell me that tomorrow, God forbid, I will break a leg. What would I gain from knowing this beforehand?" Shmerl said. "I would rather eat my Sabbath meal in peace and let God worry about tomorrow."

"Suppose someone came and told you that you were not your father's son but a bastard, and your true father was a dogcatcher? Would you be glad to learn the truth or would this enrage you?" Zeinvel asked.

"Why would I be glad? People would rather not know such an outrageous thing."

"*Nu*, so that's how it is," Zeinvel said to himself.

"But why do you waste time with such balderdash? Old bachelors and old maids have nothing better to do with their time and they dream up impossible events," Shmerl said. "Once you are happily married and you find the right business, you won't pay attention to newspapers and their silly garble."

Zeinvel did not answer. He stayed with Shmerl until Monday. Monday morning he announced that he must return to Warsaw. All of Shmerl's protests and pleadings were to no avail. Even more than Shmerl, Ruchele seemed to insist on his remaining in Reivitz. She promised to find a fitting match for him and a lucrative business. She went so far as to offer him a partnership in their haberdashery store, since they were in need of an experienced tailor and especially an honest one. Zeinvel could hardly believe his own ears. She spoke to him with the ardor and devotion of a loving sister. She besieged him to tell her the truth: Why was he so eager to return to Warsaw? Was it because of a woman?

Was he keeping a secret from his best friend? But Zeinvel knew that he could not bear to witness the deception into which Shmerl had fallen. He was also afraid that he would be unable to keep his secret forever and might eventually cause the couple's ruin. All the powers of heaven and earth seemed to conspire that he go back to Warsaw and return to his tedious job, neglected room, and bought love, and to the loneliness of one who is forced to face the bitter truth.

Translated by Deborah Menashe

The Impresario

ON MY journey to Argentina I stopped for some two weeks in Brazil. The Yiddishists were to have organized a lecture for me, but they kept postponing it. When I embarked on the boat to Santos, the sponsor had given me a large manuscript of his, apparently expecting a letter of praise. I was not in need of the lecture and neither was I willing to tell lies about his work, which I didn't like. Suddenly I had a lot of spare time on my hands.

Autumn had begun in New York, but here it was the beginning of spring. I had brought my own writings and I was working on them in my hotel room, which faced the Atlantic. Fresh breezes wafted scents of tropical plants and fruits for which I had no name in Yiddish. White sailboats rocked over the waves. They reminded me of corpses in shrouds. The sponsor of my lecture called repeatedly but I was not in a rush to respond to him. This time, after finally picking up the receiver, I heard an unfamiliar voice and the coughing and stammering of one who does not know where to begin. He was saying, "I am a devoted reader of yours. I discovered you years before anyone else. It would be a great honor for me if . . ." The man on the other end lost his tongue.

I invited him up to the room and ten minutes later he knocked at my door. I opened it and saw an emaciated man, pale, with a thin nose, sunken cheeks, and a protruding Adam's apple. He carried a little valise which I was sure was full of manuscripts. Like an experienced doctor, I made the diagnosis at first sight: He had written for years without recognition. The editors were ignorant, the publishers a bunch of money-minded fakers. Should he continue to write? I offered him a chair and he sat down, thanking me and apologizing profusely. Then I heard him say, "I have a gift for you."

"My hearty thanks," I said. Yet I heard the cynic in me saying, It's a book of poems he published himself with a dedication to his wife without whose help this work would have never been written or printed.

He took a bottle of wine and an ornate box of cookies from his valise. He mumbled something which I could not make out. My estimation of the man was completely false. He was not a poet but a professor of German and French at the University of Rio. He had deserted the Austrian Army at the time of the First World War. His father had owned an oil well in Galicia, in the region of Drohobycz. My guest's name was Alfred Reisner. He spoke an idiomatic Yiddish and had come to tell me a story and to find out why my lecture had been postponed. We became quite friendly and I said to him, "If your story is interesting, I will tell you why my lecture was postponed. But you will have to keep it a secret."

"I keep many secrets."

"Before you begin the story, may I ask you about your health? You seem frail to me, or fatigued," I said.

"What? You are mistaken, like all the others," Alfred Reisner answered. "Every time I get on a bus, passengers get up for me, even young women, as if I were a tottering old man. But I'm as strong as iron. I am in my early sixties and each day I walk between twelve and sixteen kilometers. I was never sick a day in my life. As they say, 'It should remain so for a hundred and twenty years.' However, I am not eager to live long."

"Why not?"

"You will soon know."

I called room service and ordered coffee—not the strong black coffee they drink in Brazil, but coffee with cream and sugar. We nibbled on the cookies which Alfred Reisner had brought. I heard him say, "I was afraid to call you. I have great respect for creative people. Every time I read you, I have a desire to contact you, but I never do. Why should I take up your valuable time? I hoped to meet you at the lecture here in Rio, but I knew that you would be surrounded by hordes of people. You often mention Spinoza in your stories. I imagine that he is your most beloved philosopher. Are you still a Spinozaist?"

"Not a Spinozaist, but a pantheist," I said. "Spinoza was a determinist, but I believe in free will, or *bechira*. That means . . ."

"I know what *bechira* means," Alfred Reisner said. "My father arranged for a Hebrew teacher to tutor me in the Bible and the Mishnah. When the First World War broke out and the Russians invaded Galicia, our family escaped to Vienna. My father was religious to a degree but not at all a fanatic. He was a worldly man and knew eight languages. I was born a linguist, so to speak, myself. I entered the university in Vienna, but later I was mobilized and sent to the Italian front. As I told you, I had no desire to defend the Hapsburg empire, and so I deserted."

"Is this your story?"

"Only the beginning, if you will spare me some of your time. I hope that what I want to tell you will be of interest to you. You often write on the topic of jealousy. Have you noticed that modern fiction writers ceased writing about this subject? The critics have written with so much aversion about what they call the bedroom novel that the writers have become frightened. Jealousy has become almost an anachronism in modern literature. But I always considered jealousy a mighty human and even animal instinct and the very crux of the novel. I admired Strindberg highly and read every word he wrote. The reason for this admiration was the fact that I was, and perhaps deep in my heart still am, an extremely jealous man. When I studied in the Gymnasium it was enough that my girlfriend would smile at another student for me to cut off all relations with her. I had decided to marry a virgin; if possible, one who had never dated another man. To me a man betrayed was a man defiled—a leper. You asked before if I was sick. The truth is that when I was twenty years of age I already looked old, sick, frail. I sometimes think that the fear of ending up a cuckold, and the knowledge that the whole male gender is at the mercy of women, wore me out. But my seeming frailty also helped me during the war. No one suspected me of being a deserter. Do you still want me to continue my story?" Alfred Reisner asked.

"Yes, I do."

"Well, it's very kind of you. At that time in Vienna I became involved with a young woman from the Russian part of Poland. She was three years younger than I. Her father and mother were unknown Yiddish actors who dragged around performing in stables and firehouses. Her name was Manya. She began to act with her parents when she was only five. They put on Goldfaden's and Latteiner's plays, and she also performed in some kitsch plays which her father had written. He spelled Noah with seven mistakes, as they say.

"At the time of the war Manya came to Vienna and tried to produce her father's plays. In Warsaw, a wealthy man impressed with her voice paid for her singing lessons. She eventually got a job in the opera chorus—no small achievement for a Jewish wench. Her father had died of typhoid fever in 1915. Her mother had become someone's housekeeper, and mistress as well.

"Even now, at sixty, Manya is still good-looking, but when I met her she was a rare beauty. I watched as she sang lascivious songs in a Yiddish theater to which Galician refugees came. It was a combination of a restaurant, a nightclub, and a hangout. If she came to visit late at night she always brought me a bag of leftovers. Once in a while I had to give her two crowns to pay for her fare. When she sang 'In the Holy Temple in a corner of the room sits the widow of Zion wrapped in gloom,' her voice enchanted me. It stirred up a storm in my soul. I fell passionately in love with her and was ready to marry her on the spot. But when Manya began to reveal her sexual past, it created a terrible crisis in me. I was so shattered that I felt like killing her as well as myself. By nineteen she had had a roster of over twenty lovers, among them her own father, he should roast in Gehenna. She also had some experience as a lesbian. She had tasted it all: sadism, masochism, exhibitionism, every possible perversion. She boasted to me about her sins, and despite my love, I developed a fierce hatred for her. I did not force her to confess, she did it willingly. She was proud of her lechery. Most of the men she had had were lowlifes, people of the underworld. In some cases she didn't even remember their names. Some of them were Poles connected with the Warsaw opera. She spoke to me and laughed as if the whole thing was nothing but a joke. This woman who sang so beautifully about the Holy Temple and the widow of Zion had not the slightest respect for Jewishness and Jewish history and no feeling for the Holy Land. Her body was nothing more than a piece of flesh for her to give away for the slightest favor, for a bit of flattery, or for the mere curiosity of tasting another male. She spat profanities like the shells of sunflower seeds. Millions of men fought on the fronts and died for their country, while Manya had one ambition: to become a cheap operetta singer and to sing out all the banalities with which the librettos are packed. And also to go to bed with those rich charlatans who boast about sleeping with actresses.

"While she confessed, she kissed and fondled me and tried to assure me that she was deeply in love with me, but I knew she spoke the same way to all the other men and would continue to do so to those who would come after me. I had fallen in love with a whore. That night I had a desire to leap from the bed and run. But that would have been pure suicide, since I was a deserter and Vienna was teeming with military police. To go home to my parents would endanger them, too."

Alfred Reisner took out a cigarette, rolled it between his fingers, and lit it with a lighter. "Yes, I wanted to run away from this lewd piece, but I did not run. She disgusted me, but as I kissed her and caressed her I was silly enough to demand that she be a woman like my mother and grandmother. She was so sure of her power over me that she refused even to promise. Instead she proposed marriage, with an agreement that both of us should be allowed to have others.

"What did she look like, you are wondering. She was not tall, but slim, with black hair and black eyes which expressed passion, insolence, mockery. She had an uncanny power of speech. We in Galicia speak Yiddish slightly mixed with German. But her Warsaw Yiddish had all the idioms and linguistic gems of your region. And they flowed from her mouth. When she cursed, the curses poured out like a stream of poison. When she became erotically excited, she used words at which a regiment of Cossacks would blush. I have met many cynics in my life, but Manya's cynicism was incomparable. I often played with the idea of writing down her salacious expressions, all her vulgar jokes, and then publishing them, but this plan of mine, like many others, was never realized.

"Everything came at once: the revolution in Russia, the pogroms in the Ukraine, the German defeat in France, the collapse of the Hapsburg empire. Poland became independent almost overnight and my parents demanded that I go back home with them. But after Vienna, Drohobycz looked like a hamlet, not a city. Besides, Manya wanted to go back to Warsaw, and that is where we went. The hooligans in Lemberg made a pogrom against the Jews. The trains were swarming with General Haller's soldiers, who cut Jewish beards. England came out with the Balfour Declaration and Zionism ceased being a dream. If you were in Warsaw at that time, you know what went on: a mixture of war, revolution, assassinations. First Pilsudski chased the Bolsheviks to Kiev. Then Trotsky chased the Polish Army to the Vistula, where a military miracle was supposed to have occurred. They wanted to make a Polish soldier out of me and send me to fight for my freshly hatched fatherland. But a 'miracle' happened to me, too. I acquired a passport with a false birth date.

"Jewish Warsaw was boiling like a kettle: Zionist demonstrators, Communist adventurers. We had arrived in Warsaw penniless, but Manya bumped into a former lover, a speculator, a would-be patron of the arts. His name was Zygmund Pelzer. When Zygmund kissed Manya, I became dizzy, and my heart was beating like a hammer. I knew that to live with this woman would be permanent hell for me. I swore a holy oath to get rid of her once and for all. Two weeks later, we got married.

"She had given me an ultimatum: Either get married or get out. She gave me three days to think it over. I convinced myself then that I was nothing but a miserable slave. I don't think I slept a wink those three nights.

"I once read an article of yours where you complained that the philosophers ignored the emotions and considered them a plague. Actually, the emotions are the very essence of our being. When Descartes said *Cogito, ergo sum*, he should have been talking about the emotions. Your Spinoza's adoration of adequate ideas is nothing but naïve rationalism.

"To make it short, we went to an unofficial rabbi and he filled out a *ketubah* and then set up a canopy. And who do you suppose gave away the bride? The same Zygmund Pelzer, her lover."

"How did you become a professor in Brazil?" I asked. Alfred Reisner did not answer immediately. "How did it happen? Some years later, a so-called impresario, a Pole, came from South America to Warsaw. I say 'so-called' because I've never seen him practice his profession, or any other profession, for that matter. His name is Zdizislaw Romanski, a tall blond fellow and quite a charmer. He had heard Manya sing in a trashy vaudeville theater and decided that she was exactly what he was looking for. He signed her up, took her to Brazil, and I dragged after them.

"For me to learn Portuguese was easy, since I knew Latin and French. A position was open at the University of Rio for an assistant professor of German and I was hired. In time I began to teach French, too. Manya could have become rich with her voice, but the charlatan, the impresario, invaded her life and my life as well. It began on the ship to Brazil.

"Two things I have learned in my life of disgrace. First, that the whole concept of free will, free choice, and all other phrases about human freedom are sheer nonsense. Man has no more freedom than a bedbug. In this respect, Spinoza was right. However, consistent determinist that he was, he had no reason to preach ethics. The second thing I have learned is that, under certain circumstances, every human passion can reverse itself and become the very opposite of what it was. From a psychological point of view, Hegel was right: Each thesis proceeds in the direction of its antithesis. The mightiest love can become the most venomous hatred. A wild anti-Semite can become an ardent lover of the Jews or even a convert to Judaism. A miser can suddenly begin to throw all his money around. A pacifist can become a murderer. The man who sits before you lived through many metamorphoses. One time I was burning with jealousy. The mere thought that my wife could have the slightest desire for another man drove me to insanity. A few years later, I came to the point where I could lie with Manya and her lover in one bed.

Please don't ask me for any details or explanations. Pleasure itself is a form of suffering. Asceticism and hedonism are actually synonymous. I know that I am not revealing anything new to you. Our religious sages knew about it in their way."

"What kind of person was this impresario?" I asked.

"A demon."

"How old was he?"

"Who knows how old a demon is? A true word never came out of his mouth—a psychopathic liar, a crazy boaster. According to him, all the beauties in Poland were his concubines, Pilsudski and his generals were all on a first-name basis with him. In the war with the Bolsheviks he managed to perform all kinds of heroic acts and he received countless medals. As far as I could tell, he never served in the military. Neither was he descended from counts and barons. His father was nothing but a notary public in Wolhynia.

"After all I have been through, nothing astonishes me anymore. Nevertheless, whenever I have the feeling that he can no longer surprise us, he does something which baffles me completely. His physical strength was and still is extraordinary. Although he is the worst alcoholic I've known, I have never known him to be ill. According to medical theory, he should have burned out his stomach and his bowels by now. Every morning when he opens his eyes, he repeats the same joke, 'I'm going to gargle with mouthwash,' and the mouthwash is a tea glass of vodka on an empty stomach. He turned Manya into a drunkard also. He continually threatens Manya and me with suicide, or that he is going to kill both of us. He also babbles about converting to Judaism."

"Who pays the bills?" I asked.

"I do."

"Didn't he ever try to do anything?"

"Only when he was sure to fail."

"Would you call yourself a masochist?" I asked.

"As good a name as any. Yes, me, them, and the whole human race; its wars, revolutions, arts, even its religions. Humanity is nothing but a permanent rebellion against God and what Spinoza called the order of things, or nature. Man was born a slave, and with the bitterness of a slave. He has to do the opposite of what he is forced to do. He is God's eternal opposition: actually Satan."

"Do you believe that your impresario is still in love with Manya?" I asked.

Alfred Reisner seemed to shudder. "In love? Who knows what love is? The whole notion of love is vague and ambiguous. But when you are dealing with a demon, what kind of love is he capable of? He destroyed her. She calls him 'my angel of death.' She drank until she lost her voice. She has a throat disease which the doctors in Brazil cannot identify, a type of cancer. Quite often she becomes dangerously sick and we have to take her to the hospital. She gets asthma and loses the power of speech. Once, she coughed so terribly I had to rush her to the hospital, and they discovered a collapsed lung.

"It all came as a result of drinking, screaming, trying to sing without a voice, pushing the body to be young when it was ordered to be old. These two have waged a twenty-year war, a bitter war, a war of madness and mutiny. Unbelievable as it sounds, I haven't figured out in all these years what they are fighting about. You forget such things, like a nightmare. Both of them rave at the same time, she in Yiddish and he in Polish. They carry on unrelated monologues. I've often thought that if one could record their wild conversations, it would be material for a literary masterpiece. Different as we are, all three of us have one common quality: we have not the slightest knack for practical matters. When a fuse blows in our home, we sit there in the dark for hours helplessly waiting for the superintendent, who is a drunk himself and never available. We lose money, we forget dates, we are constantly in a state of utter confusion. A day doesn't pass when something doesn't break down in our caricature of a house: the electricity, the gas, the toilet, the telephone. When it rains, the water leaks right through the roof into the bedroom and we have to cover the floor with buckets. Yes, you can call us masochists. But why just the three of us? And what miserable fate keeps us together year after year after year? We have given ourselves the holiest oaths to part once and for all and put an end to this tragicomedy of an existence. We have actually run away from each other the devil knows how many times and under the most bizarre circumstances, but we always come back to the same mess, the same madness, drawn by a power for which I haven't yet found a name in any dictionary, encyclopedia, you name it. Neither Freud nor Adler nor Jung could have ever explained it by their various theories. Passion? You can call it passion, complex, insanity, or simply meshuggas. We leave and we get sick from yearning and brooding. We write desperate letters to one another and plead for peace, forgiveness, a fresh start, and other ridiculous banalities of which we make fun ourselves. We laugh and cry and spit when we meet again and we drink a toast to our mutual dybbuk. Yes, I too have learned to drink, although not as much as they. I could not afford it. I have a family to provide for, woe is me."

Alfred Reisner glanced at his wristwatch and said, "It is later than I thought. Please forgive me for taking up so much of your precious time. To whom could I tell a story like this? There are philosophers, psychologists, and even those who consider themselves writers at the university, but to confide in them would be sheer suicide. Apart from the office girl who sends my salary every month, no one knows my address. Now that I'm as good as retired, I'm as good as a corpse. Well, how about your lecture? When will it take place?"

"I'm afraid it won't," I said.

"Could you tell me the reason?"

The telephone rang and the sponsor told me that my lecture had been rescheduled. He gave me the date. I conveyed the news to my guest, and for a moment his eyes lit up.

"These are good tidings. It will be an event. We will come to hear you. All three of us."

"The Pole also?" I asked.

Alfred Reisner thought it over. "Since he is really not of this world, who knows whether he is a Pole, a

Russian, or a Jew? He is a great admirer of yours. He reads you in English and in French. A little bit in Yiddish, too. Don't be afraid. He won't come to the lecture riding on a broom, with a tail and horns. When he needs to, he can be a perfect gentleman."

Translated by the author

Logarithms

THAT SABBATH afternoon the talk turned to a merchant who set fire to his store in order to obtain the insurance money. I heard Aunt Yentl say, "Well, arson is arson. It was done before him and it will be done after him. Easy money is an evil temptation. All he had to do was pour some kerosene on the merchandise and light a match. The insurance company adjusters pretend to take the merchant at his word. It's not their own money they're paying; it all comes from the banks in Petersburg. In olden times, when a merchant could not repay a debt, they took possession of his house and business or the man was imprisoned. People went to jail for such deeds. Today one can easily declare bankruptcy. At the worst, one sets a fire. If luck is on his side, he'll be released in no time or he can run off to America."

"Just the same," our neighbor Bela Zyvia said, "to

risk burning a whole marketplace, and half a town to boot, one needs the heart of a murderer."

"Women, this is not a subject for the Sabbath," Aunt Yentl said.

I heard my Aunt Yentl make this statement almost every Saturday, but she frequently broke her own rule to keep the Sabbath pure and gay and told stories which had the scent of gossip. She would tap her own lips and say, "Be quiet, my mouth" or, "Don't let me sin with my own words, Father in heaven."

Aunt Yentl went to the kitchen to bring refreshments. She returned with a tray containing cherries, plums, and a drink called kvass, and said, "A man himself is his own worst enemy. A hundred enemies cannot do to a person the damage he is capable of doing to himself." She sat down, stroking the colored ribbons which hung from the top of her bonnet and the golden earrings which dangled from her earlobes, and I knew she was about to tell a story.

Aunt Yentl drank some kvass and wet her lips with the tip of her tongue. After some hesitation, she began: "True, it is not a story for the Sabbath, but there is a lesson to be learned from it. When I lived with my first husband—he should intercede for all of us—in the town of Krasnystaw, we had as a neighbor a widow from Lublin named Chaya Keila. Her husband left her with a gifted son, Yossele. He knew half the Pentateuch by heart by the age of five. He was also a mathematical wizard. His father had left him a book entitled *The Study of Algebra*, and little Yossele pored over it day and night. His mother took him from house to house to show off his remarkable talent. He had calculated how many drops of water filled the town river. He asserted that in the dense forest behind the squire's castle there were two trees with an identical number of leaves, though no one had ever counted them. People gaped in astonishment. Chaya Keila was in constant fear that the neighbors might give him the evil eye. Every two days, she took him to an old woman who knew how to exorcise malicious spirits. Before the beginning of every month, she gave the boy herbs to purge him of worms in his intestines. She had learned incantations written on parchment by the Preacher of Kozienice. Once, when Yossele became sick with fever, an old witch told the mother to dig a ditch behind the house, dress the sick boy in white linen, and make him lie in the ditch to fool the angel of death into thinking he was already buried in his shroud. When the rabbi heard about this, he sent his beadle to knock at her shutter and warn the frightened mother that this was an act of sorcery. Yes, overly protective mothers do bizarre things. The rabbi told the mother to give the boy two new names—Chaim and Alter, meaning 'life' and 'old age.' The mother called him by these two names for years, but strangers forgot them and still called him Yossele.

"I will make it short: Yossele grew up to be a genius in Torah and mathematics. At that time there was a Gentile apothecary in town who knew Latin better than most priests. Once when Chaya Keila brought Yossele to buy pills, the two conversed and suddenly the apothecary cried out to Chaya Keila, 'Congratulations, your son has already learned logarithms without a teacher.'

"I had never heard this word when his mother came running to our house with the good tidings. She repeated this difficult word so many times that I learned how to pronounce it myself. For weeks Chaya Keila spoke about nothing but logarithms—'logarithms this,' and 'logarithms that!'

"Later Yossele learned how to play chess. He could beat all the town's chess players, Jews and Gentiles alike. He played chess with the apothecary's daughter, Helena, who smoked cigarettes and was as clever as a man. He even played with the Russian chief of police and with some Polish dignitaries. A few insisted on playing for money with the boy, thus helping his widowed mother make ends meet. Every day the mother announced the boy's latest victories. The squire of the town, who was a count, presented Yossele with a chessboard and figures made of ivory, after Yossele went so far as to checkmate the magistrate himself.

"Now listen to this: There was in our town a rich Jew named Wolf Markus, a timber merchant. From the Poles impoverished by the revolution, he bought large parcels of forest and let the trees, mostly oaks, be chopped down. In order to estimate how much lumber could be made from them, one needed mathematics. When Wolf Markus heard of Yossele's knowledge, he invited him to his house and they discussed logarithms for hours with Wolf's bookkeeper. Everyone present knew mathematics and they all played chess, even Wolf's two daughters, Serele and Blumele. They all became enthusiastic about Yossele's scholarship and wisdom.

"Serele fell in love with him at first sight, as they say. He had come for an hour and conquered the world. In a small town everyone knows what's cooking in other people's pots. Chaya Keila came running to us immediately with the good tidings. But why elaborate? Wolf Markus had accumulated large dowries for his daughters and he spoke openly of his intentions. Fathers, even more than mothers, are eager to marry off their daughters. One day he spoke to Yossele of a match, and the next they wrote preliminary agreements. Two weeks later, all the relatives on both sides were invited to the engagement party. The town was boiling like a kettle. Wolf Markus went to Lublin and came back with a golden watch for Yossele. The boy was no longer his mother's son, but Wolf's. Chaya Keila laughed and cried from happiness. She almost died of fear that someone would snatch away her good fortune. I was invited to the celebration and I heard of the gifts Yossele would get—the golden watch, a silver watch, a Pentateuch in silk, a set of Mishnah bound in leather, an embroidered prayer shawl, and a fox-fur hat with thirteen tails. The one who wrote out the marriage contract had his own style, and got a percentage of everything he wrote. Chaya Keila had jewelry left from her own marriage and she gave it to the bride for signing the agreement, as was the custom. If someone had suggested she offer her head, she would not have hesitated a moment.

"It looked as if Yossele had fallen into a bed of clover,

and the city reverberated with envy. Other mothers had also wanted to make brilliant matches for their daughters. Chaya Keila cursed them in advance. I heard her say, 'Was it my fault that I gave birth to a genius? It is written somewhere that the womb of a woman is like a drawer. Whatever you put in, you take out. Yossele's father, he should rest in peace, was a scholar himself. He had a great mind, and the apple does not fall far from the tree. But no one can lock people's mouths. They always search for something malicious, never for anything good.'

"I remember it all," Aunt Yentl said. "Envious people just could not stand it that a Jewish young man understood logarithms and married a rich man's daughter. It is written in the holy books that because of hatred and envy Jerusalem was destroyed. I was still a young girl then, but I was afraid that something terrible would happen to Yossele. The evil tongues went from house to house and maligned him. Even though he was a relative of mine, the evil tongues came to our house— but I am forgetting the main thing: Wolf Markus arranged for a wedding which cost him a fortune. He even brought musicians from Janok and Zamosc. Of course, he could not invite everybody, and those who were omitted burned with rage. Since Yossele had the name of a scholar, they called him up for the reading of the Torah, which was a sign of respect. And this inflamed the gossips even more.

"Now not far from Krasnystaw, in the town of Schebrshin, lived a Jew, Jacob Reifman. People considered him both a scholar and a heretic. He did not deny God, but it was said that he wrote books in German and sent them to the Maskilim—the enlightened Jews in Germany. The Hasidim and the Maskilim waged war among themselves, and the word was that Yossele and Reifman exchanged scholarly letters and made fun of the Hasidic rabbis. A yeshiva boy in our town spread the rumor that Yossele said that those who built the Holy Temple made mistakes in measuring the columns, the sacred vessels, and the altar. Immediately there arose in town a hue and cry that Yossele considered himself cleverer than King Solomon. When Chaya Keila heard this accusation, she was ill with fear. She came running to our house, crying bitterly that her enemies were trying to tear the crown from her head.

"One Sabbath, there was pandemonium in town. When Yossele was called up as the third one to the Torah for special honors, a stranger ran up to the reading table and tried to shove him away, screaming that Yossele was an apostate and a betrayer of Israel, who should be excommunicated with the blowing of the shofar in the light of black candles. Chaya Keila had come that Saturday to the women's section of the synagogue to pray. These vicious words about her beloved son made her utter a terrible scream, and she fell to the floor with a heart seizure. They tried to revive her with Yom Kippur drops, and massaged her temples, but it was all in vain. She was carried out on the stretcher which always stood at the door of the poorhouse. This was no longer a Sabbath but a day of mourning and fasting.

In the bedlam which followed, butchers, coachmen, and horse dealers rushed into the synagogue and attacked the intruder who had reviled Yossele. The readings of the Torah and the prayers were stopped immediately. The squire heard of the outburst, and a fear fell upon all the Jews. The community leaders had to send negotiators to apologize to the squire for the violence at the synagogue and pay a fine for the scandal.

" 'Excommunication' is a word which creates fear even among the Gentiles. For generations such a thing never took place in Poland except when the false Messiah, Jacob Frank, converted with his wife and disciples and proclaimed in open court that the Jews used Christian blood for their matzohs. This didn't happen in my time, but I heard about it."

"But what happened to Yossele?" Bela Zyvia asked.

Aunt Yentl shook her head. "I don't like to say it on the Sabbath," she said, "but something terrible—even unbelievable."

"What was it?"

"He changed his gold coin," Aunt Yentl said.

"You mean he converted?"

"He went to the priest and married Helena, the daughter of the apothecary."

"He left his wife?" my mother asked.

"His wife, God, the Jews," Aunt Yentl answered.

"Did he divorce his wife?" my mother asked.

"The wife of a convert does not need a divorce," Aunt Yentl said.

"Yentl, you are mistaken," my mother said. "According to the law, a convert remains a Jew and his wife is considered a married woman and she needs divorce papers if she intends to remarry."

"This is the first time I've heard that," Bela Zyvia said.

"If one lives long enough, one hears many things for the first time," Aunt Yentl said. "Men look strong, but they are actually very weak."

"Well, this is the law of the Torah," my mother said. "I know of a case where one of the rebels who tried to overthrow the Czar converted while in prison. They had to bring a rabbi to the jail, and a scribe and two witnesses, and he divorced his Jewish wife according to the law of Moses and Israel while in prison. Men! What betrayers men are!"

"The Torah is like the ocean," Aunt Yentl said. "There is no bottom. Women, it's getting late. The sun is setting. We soon have to recite 'God of Abraham.'"

I turned my face to the west. The sun was setting, surrounded with glowing clouds. They reminded me of the river of fire where the wicked are punished in Gehenna. For a long while the women sat silently, with bowed heads, wiping their noses into their aprons. Then I heard Aunt Yentl reciting: "God of Abraham, Isaac, and Jacob, protect the poor people of Israel and Thine own glory. The Holy Sabbath is going away and the lovely week should come now. It should be with Torah and good deeds, riches and honor, charity and mercy. An end should come to the dark exile. The sound of Elijah's shofar should be heard and the Messiah, our redeemer, should come speedily and in our days. Amen selah."

"Amen selah," all the women answered in one voice.

"I see three stars in the sky," Aunt Yentl said. "I think one is now allowed to light a candle, but where are my matches? Every Friday when I light the candles I put away the matches, but they get lost. Old age is not a joy."

There was suddenly light. Aunt Yentl had found her matches. I looked up to the sky and saw that the moon had appeared with its face of Joshua, the son of Nun. My mother stood up and looked at me angrily, almost with contempt. Was it because I, too, was a man and might one day betray womankind as Yossele did? I had promised her many times not to come to Aunt Yentl's on the Sabbath, but her Sabbath fruit and stories were too great a temptation for me. I could not understand why I felt a great compassion arise in me for Yossele and something like a desire to know Helena, play chess with her, and learn logarithms. I remembered my brother Joshua in a quarrel saying to my father, "The other nations studied and learned, made discoveries in mathematics, physics, chemistry, astronomy, but we Jews remained stuck on a little law of an egg which was laid on a holiday." I also remembered my father answering, "This little law contains more wisdom than all the discoveries the idolaters have made since the time of Abraham."

Translated by the author and Lester Goran

Gifts

I MET him near the bank where I cashed a check I
received from a Yiddish newspaper. I was a young
writer and he—I will call him Max Blendever—was
known as a Zionist leader in Warsaw and a councilman
at the City Hall. He had quarreled with the major
Zionist group and had become the head of a faction of
extremists who called themselves revisionists. I recognized him from his pictures in the Yiddish press. He
was of medium height, broad-shouldered, with a large
head, high cheekbones, and thick eyebrows. I have
noticed that politicians are inclined to let their eyebrows
grow, most probably to appear more masculine or to
hide their sly eyes. Max Blendever was known as a
fighter. In the city council he assailed the anti-Semites
violently. He had enemies not only among the Gentiles
but also among the Jews who contended that he was
too aggressive and did damage with his attacks.

As a rule, I would never have stopped a stranger in the street, especially not a famous man. But I had recently heard that his wife, Carola, had died in a car accident. This woman, whom I had never met, had sent me a New Year's card and a bottle of Carmel wine on the eve of Rosh Hashanah. The gift arrived at the address of the journal where I was a proofreader. It was a complete surprise to me. Was Carola Blendever a Yiddishist? Did she read me in the little magazines that never had more than a few hundred readers? As far as I knew, most of the wives of the Zionist leaders were half assimilated. I wanted to send the husband a condolence card when she passed away, but did nothing about it. I was one of those who considered him too arrogant. We Jews, I believed, should not forget that we are a minority in every country in the world, and should act accordingly.

But now that I encountered him face to face, I went over to him and said, "You don't know me, but everyone knows you. My name is . . ."

"I know you, I've heard of you," Max Blendever replied. He pulled the cigar out from between his lips, extended his hand to me, and shook mine vigorously. He said, "My late wife mentioned your name once in a while. I am a politician, not a writer. Besides, I am for Hebrew, not for Yiddish, but I buy Yiddish books and journals. They are sent to me from time to time. In what direction are you walking? Perhaps you can accompany me part of the way. You have certainly heard about the misfortune with my wife."

"Yes. I'm terribly sorry. I received a gift from her. I could not understand where she heard about me and why I deserved it."

Max Blendever, who walked so quickly that I could barely keep up with him, suddenly stopped.

"A gift, huh? What sort of gift?"

"A bottle of Carmel wine."

Something like an angry smile appeared on his face. He measured me from head to toe. "You were not the only one," he said. "People have different passions. Some smoke opium, others take hashish. There are those whose greatest pleasure is to run in the forests and hunt bears or wolves. My Carola, may she rest in peace, had a passion for sending gifts. I was a poor boy when I married her, but she was a rich daughter. She received a handsome dowry and she spent it all on gifts."

We walked for a while in silence. Max Blendever took long strides. At Marszalkowsky Boulevard, he glanced around and said, "Now that I've begun telling you about her, maybe you would like to go with me to a café? Let's drink a glass of coffee together."

"It would be an honor and a pleasure," I answered.

"What is the honor? Each of us does his own work, right or wrong. God will judge us, if He exists. And if He doesn't exist, it is too bad. If you don't drink coffee, you can take a glass of tea, cocoa, or whatever you prefer. I like black coffee without cream or sugar."

We went to a café, and it was half empty in the middle of the day. A waiter came right over to our table. Max Blendever ordered black coffee for himself and tea with lemon for me.

He relit his cigar with a lighter and said, "Since you are a fiction writer, or plan to become one, you must be interested in people's character and their idiosyncrasies. I always knew that different types of philanthropists existed in the world. American millionaires give away fortunes for the most bizarre causes. One millionairess in Chicago, a spinster, left two million dollars to her poodle. But my Carola's passion to send gifts, often to complete strangers, was something new to me. She never told me about them, although I heard her speak about various presents. I thought this was the way rich women behaved. With them, every emotion must be expressed in concrete terms. Having had little experience with the so-called beautiful sex, I left her to her own devices. You are looking at a man who never had another woman aside from his lawful wife. For me, affairs were only a waste of time. I had the illusion that all females were more or less alike."

"If only I could have such an illusion," I said.

"My real passion was politics. It began when I was still a boy. From childhood on, I always heard Jews lamenting about their fate to live in exile. I thought to myself, What can come from all this moaning and sighing? Why not do something? And this is how I became what I am today. My father taught me that a Jew must bow his head when people abuse him and offer the other cheek. This was sheer nonsense to me. But let me return to my story. Maybe you could even write about it someday; but don't mention my name."

"I certainly wouldn't."

"Yes, my wife. I had, as they say, one God and one

wife. I loved her and believe she loved me, too. But her mania of sending gifts baffled me. Of course she also had a buying mania. You cannot give gifts without buying them first. I sometimes think that her drive to buy things was her number-one passion. I could never take a walk with her without her window-shopping. Once, we were walking in the vicinity of the Catholic cemetery in Powazek and passed a store which displayed coffins, and sure enough, she stopped to stare at them. I asked her, 'Do you want to buy a coffin? You know that Jews don't bury their dead in coffins, at least not here in Poland.' But you could not tear her away from a store window. I tell you this to show how compulsive her buying mania was. I learned about her obsession for gifts later. Let me make it short. Every year she sent gifts to hundreds of men, women, and children. She only waited for an excuse to celebrate some event, a holiday, a birthday, an engagement party, a wedding, a circumcision, you name it. I found a notebook where she listed countless candidates and occasions for her benefactions. She had given away virtually her entire inheritance. As you can imagine, I was often on the road—congresses, conferences, an endless number of party meetings. You know our Jewish organizations. Every party has its factions, and sooner or later every faction splits. Here in Warsaw we have a leftist politician, a certain Dr. Bruk, who has already been everything in his life: a Bundist, a Communist, a member of the right Labor Zionists, the left Labor Zionists, an anarchist, a Sejmist, a territorialist. His last party split so many times it became a faction of a faction of a faction. A joke is told that when his present remnant of a party decides to hold a general meeting, instead of a hall they hire a droshky pulled by a single horse.

"Needless to say, a man with my temperament and my big mouth has no lack of enemies. It cannot be any other way. But in the last few years I began to realize that my enemies had somehow become more lenient than they used to be. Even when they attacked me, they did it, so to speak, with kid gloves. Their arguments were mollified with bits of praise. Here and there they even pointed out some of my merits. What happened? Why have they become so charitable toward me? I wondered. Do they consider me so old and far gone that I am altogether harmless? Or have my opponents grown slightly civilized in their old age? I was too busy to ponder it. Yes, you guessed it! Carola had decided that I didn't have enough friends for her barrage of gifts and began sending presents to my enemies.

"When I found out about it I raised hell. It was the first and last time I spoke about divorce. I knew none of my enemies could ever have believed that Carola had done all this without my knowledge. They were all convinced that the wolf had become a lamb and decided to pad his career with bribery. I screamed so that our neighbors came running. My wife had entirely destroyed the little reputation I had built up in a lifetime. She had completely ruined me. How do they say it? A thousand enemies cannot do more harm to a man than a well-meaning wife. I say well meaning, because when my anger subsided (how long can someone rage and break plates?) and I tried to explain to her what a catastrophe all this was for me, she swore that she could not understand why I made such a fuss. 'What is so terrible about showing a little good will? Your enemies actually have the same goal as you: to help the Jews. It is only that their approach is different.'

"My dear young man, I don't know myself why I'm confiding all this to you. Until now, I haven't told it to anyone. After brooding over it a long time and eating my heart out, I made peace with the fact that the damage was done. What could I do? Write letters to all my adversaries explaining that my wife sent them gifts without my consent? I would only make myself ridiculous. I decided to do what I believed was my duty and that what my enemies thought of me or said did not matter. I can only tell you that out of all the gifts the bottle of wine she sent to you was the most sensible. You are a young writer and have nothing to do with politics. But to send a Christmas gift to the greatest anti-Semite in Poland—Adam Nowaczynski—is an act that absolutely borders on madness."

"She did that?" I asked.

"Yes, exactly. The irony of it is that this deranged Jew-baiter wrote her an exceptionally friendly letter where he praised the Jews to heaven. He wrote, more or less, that he maligns the Jews only because he knows how intelligent they are, what sharp minds they have developed by studying the Talmud, and how dangerous their competition is for the naïve and gullible Poles, who can be outsmarted so easily. Let us find a way to utilize our respective potentials for the common good of all

Polish citizens, and so on and so on. Like all dema-
gogues, he believed his own lies."

"Giving presents is not something new in our history," I said. "When Jacob heard that his brother Esau
was coming to meet him with four hundred armed
ruffians, he sent a gift which would have been worth a
treasure today."

"Yes. Yes. Yes. The weaker ones always try to
curry favor, but it doesn't help for long," Max Blendever said. "They take what you give them, embrace you,
kiss you, call you brother, and a little later they assault
you again. The truth is that Carola did not do this to
help the Jews; it was nothing but her addiction to gifts.
Freud would have interpreted it with hair-splitting
casuistry, most probably with some newly discovered
gift complex. He and his disciples must rationalize every
sort of human peculiarity. But in what lousy book is it
written that everything can be explained? My theory
is, *nothing can be explained*."

"That is also my theory," I said. "When literature
goes too far into explanations and commentaries, it becomes tedious and false."

"Yes, right," Max Blendever agreed. "Your tea has
gotten cold. May I order you a glass of hot tea?"

"Thank you, no. Definitely not."

"Why not?" Max Blendever asked.

"This, too, could never be explained."

Translated by Deborah Menashe

Runners to Nowhere

THE TWO of us, Zeinvel Markus and I, were sitting in Rector's cafeteria on Broadway drinking coffee and eating rice pudding. The conversation turned to the period from 1939 to 1945, the Hitler war and the destruction of Warsaw. In those years I lived in the United States, but he, Zeinvel Markus, remained in Warsaw and went through all the terrors of the Second World War. In Warsaw, Zeinvel Markus had been a columnist of the kind we called a "feuilletonist." His columns, featured at the bottom of the page, were somewhat clever, a little sentimental, and used many quotations from writers and philosophers. He especially loved to quote Nietzsche. As far as I knew, Zeinvel Markus had never married. He was small and had yellowish skin and slanted eyes. He used to joke that he was a great-grandchild of Genghis Khan and the daughter of a rabbi, one of his captive concubines. Zeinvel Markus suffered from at least a dozen imaginary illnesses, among them impotence. He both complained of and boasted about this malady, at the same time hinting about his great success with German maidens. He was for many years the Berlin correspondent of a Yiddish newspaper in Warsaw. He had returned to Warsaw from Germany at the beginning of the thirties and we remained friends until I left for America.

Zeinvel Markus arrived in the United States in 1948 from Shanghai, where he had managed to live as a refugee for some time. In New York he developed a new version of impotence—a literary one. He suffered from writer's cramp in his right hand. For some reason, the editors of the Yiddish press in America had little preference for his ambiguous aphorisms and quotations from Nietzsche, Kierkegaard, Spengler, and Georg Kaiser. He also developed a sickness which seemed to me genuine—abdominal ulcers. The doctors forbade him to smoke and allowed him to drink no more than two cups of coffee a day. However, Zeinvel Markus said to me, "Without coffee my life isn't worth a pinch of tobacco. I'm not going to become an American Methuselah anyhow."

Zeinvel Markus had countless stories to tell, and I never got tired of spending time with him. He knew personally all the so-called professional Jews in the whole world. He had visited Baron Hirsch's Jewish colonies in Argentina, had gone to all the Zionist congresses, and traveled to South Africa, Australia, Ethiopia, and Persia. They translated his feuilletons in the Hebrew press in Tel Aviv. I tried many times to persuade him to write his memoirs, and as usual Zeinvel Markus answered me with a paradox: "All memoirs are full of lies, and since I can tell only the truth, how can I write my memoirs?"

That afternoon, as always when we met, we finally began to speak of love, fidelity, treachery, and Zeinvel said, "In my life I've seen at least a thousand forms of treachery, but the treachery of the two runners I never even imagined before 1939."

"Runners?" I asked. "What do you mean by runners?"

"I mean a man and a woman in the process of running," Zeinvel replied. "Wait a moment, I'm going to bring us two cups of coffee."

"I've had enough coffee already," I said.

"You will drink another. If you don't drink it, I will," Zeinvel said. "In Russia, even under the Bolsheviks, one could get a glass of hot coffee, but here in the golden land you cannot get a *hot* cup of coffee for love or money. It's not only in this cafeteria. You can't get a cup of really hot coffee even in the Waldorf-Astoria. I tried in Washington, in Chicago, in San Francisco, but to no avail. There is such a thing as collective insanity. Wait, I will be back in a moment."

I saw Zeinvel pick up an empty tray from an adjoining table and dash to the counter. Immediately he came back. "Where's my check?" he asked. "In this cafeteria if you lose your check there's only one way out for you, suicide."

"Zeinvel," I said, "you are holding the check in your hand."

"What? I'm really getting confused in America, perhaps I'm senile."

I noticed that as he went to the counter he picked up a newspaper which someone had left on a chair. He returned with two cups of coffee and an egg cookie. The newspaper was yesterday's. I touched one of the cups and said, "Zeinvel, this cup is really hot. What do you say now?"

"The cup, not the coffee," Zeinvel said. "This is an American trick: they make the dishes hot and leave the contents cold. The American does not believe in such a thing as objective truth. The judge in an American court is not interested in whether the accused is guilty or not guilty. All he cares about is whether his defense is faultless or not. This is also true of the female sex. A woman doesn't want to be beautiful, she only wants to *look* beautiful. If she wears the right makeup, then she's a beauty. When Adam and Eve discovered that they were naked, Eve immediately began to sew a fig leaf to hide it."

"Who were the runners?" I asked.

Zeinvel gave me a puzzled look, as if he didn't immediately understand my words. "Oh yes, the runners. They ran away from Hitler. It happened when the radio announced that everyone in Warsaw should hurry across the Praga Bridge and run to the part of Poland which Molotov and Ribbentrop had divided among themselves. Bombs were falling in Warsaw. Buildings had collapsed and one could see corpses protruding from the rubble. The new dictator, Rydz-Śmigly, Pilsudski's heir, was as much a general as I'm a Turk. All he had was an ornate cap with a shining visor. The Poles and the Jews are as far apart as the sky is from the earth but both are cursed with the same mad optimism. The Jews are sure that the Almighty, who is actually an anti-Semite, loves them more than anything else in the universe, and the Poles believe in the power of their mustaches. The Polish general staff did not possess more than brass medals and curly mustaches in those days. Their soldiers went out to fight Hitler's tanks with swords and horses, as in the times of King Sobieski. Their leaders twirled their mustaches and up until the last minute kept on assuring everybody that victory was on their side.

"I lived in a little hotel on Mylno Street. This alley was so well hidden that no one could find it, not even the letter carrier. When I heard the announcement on the radio, I took a satchel and began to run. I knew that it was beyond my strength to carry a valise in this pandemonium. I saw men running with trunks that would have been too heavy even for a camel."

Zeinvel tasted the coffee and winced. "Ice cold."

"What happened to the runners?" I asked.

"One of them you knew quite well: Feitl Porysover, the playwright. Perhaps you also knew his wife, Tsvetl."

"He had a wife?" I asked.

"It seems he married after you left for America," Zeinvel said. "As you know, Feitl had a squeaky voice, and he managed to give all his protagonists the same tone of voice. He tried to imitate Chekhov. Chekhov's heroes whisper and sigh constantly, and Feitl's chirped like the cricket behind my grandfather's stove. You remember that Feitl was small, even smaller than I am, but his wife, Tsvetl, was an aspiring actress, a giant of a woman with the voice of a man. Feitl must have promised her leading roles in his plays. He, too, got nothing but promises. Hermann, the director, assured him every year that he would produce one of his masterpieces. As to Hermann, he had a promise from a theatrical angel that he would finance his productions. It was all a chain of promises. That angel was a swindler and a bankrupt. I've forgotten his name. My memory plays hide-and-seek with me. When I need it, it's not there, and when I don't need it, it reminds me of thousands of mingy trivialities, especially at night when I cannot fall asleep.

"What was I saying? Yes, we were running. There were few women among the runners, but Tsvetl was there and also Feitl. He was carrying a valise full of plays and she carried a box full of women's garments and a huge basket of food. She ran and she ate—whole sausages, Swiss cheese, cans of sardines and herrings. She had long legs and ran quickly, but Feitl, that shlemiel, followed with his tiny steps. She ate everything herself and gave him nothing. He called after her with his shrill voice and begged her not to rush, but she played dumb. We all had to run, because any moment Nazi planes could come and destroy us with their guns.

"When we started out, everyone was laden with luggage, but in time they had to drop it. The road was full of abandoned bundles, baskets, sacks, bags. Someone told me that when Feitl realized he couldn't go much farther with his valise, he stopped and began to choose those plays he thought were his best and threw the others away. It would have been terribly comic if it hadn't been so tragic—an author having to decide in the hubbub of running where his immortality might lie. I was told that in the end he was left with only one play, the pages of which he placed in his pockets. Peasants from the villages, their wives and their children, picked up the loot, but no one was eager for Feitl's manuscripts.

"Now listen. A so-called Yiddish poet also ran among this crowd. He often appeared on the literary scene in Warsaw after you left for America. His name was Bentze Zotlmacher, a fellow from the provinces, a big boor, with the face of a boxer and a bush of hair which stood up like wires. In the Writers' Club they used to organize a lot of literary evenings in the late thirties, all for the so-called progressives. You know that there were very few proletarians among the Jews in Poland, and Jewish peasants did not exist at all. But in the poems which these scribblers wrote, all three million Jews in Poland were either workers in factories or peasants. All those writers predicted the imminent social revolution and the dictatorship of the proletariat. The last two or three years before the war, a number of Trotskyites had emerged. The Stalinists and the Trotskyites waged violent battles and called one another Fascists, enemies of the people, provocateurs, imperialists. They kept on threatening one another that when the masses rose in the streets all the traitors would be hung from lamp-posts. The Stalinists would hang the Trotskyites, the Trotskyites would hang the Stalinists, and both would hang the general Zionists, the right Poale Zionists, the left Poale Zionists, and, of course, all pious Jews. I remember that the president of the Yiddish Club, Dr. Gottleib, once asked in a debate, "Where will they find so many lampposts in Warsaw?"

"Bentze had been a Stalinist first, then he became a Trotskyite. Poetry was not enough for him. He had a pair of huge paws, and when the Stalinists heckled him, he ran down from the stage and gave them mighty blows. He often got a beating himself, and went around with a bandaged head. For curiosity's sake I once listened to his recitation: the usual clichés and banalities. In that day of escaping from Warsaw, Bentze Zotlmacher proved to be the best runner of all. He carried on his back two huge rucksacks and in his hands two large valises. He seemed to have prepared himself for the task days in advance. However, since we were all running to the part of Poland that belonged to Russia, which meant to Stalin, Bentze Zotlmacher realized his dilemma: he had bet on the wrong side. The city of Bialystok, to which we were all running, was full of Russians. The Warsaw Stalinists ran in a separate group ready to take over power the moment they crossed the frontier. Someone said that Bentze would have had a better chance to remain alive among the Nazis in Warsaw than in Bialystok among his former comrades.

"Since I had taken almost no luggage, and what I had taken I abandoned even before we reached the bridge, I was unburdened and could walk quickly, almost as quickly as Bentze. I witnessed two curious events, first how Bentze while running tried to make up to the Stalinists. It didn't take him long. He switched over with shameless vulgarity. He had many packs of cigarettes and he offered cigarettes only to the Stalinists. Rarely was anyone able to take cigarettes with them in that turmoil, but Bentze was well prepared. When a Trotskyite asked him for a cigarette, he answered loudly so everyone could hear him that he didn't want to have any traffic with the Trotskyite traitors to the masses, lackeys of Rockefeller and Hearst, agents of the Fascists. I expected that the Stalinists would reject this false neophyte, but here I was mistaken. For politicians it is a natural thing that one converts to the strong side without any preliminaries. They themselves, the Stalinists, had already made similar conversions. Since Bentze spat on the Trotskyites and poured praise on Comrade Stalin, they began to treat him like one of their own. The *Homo politico* is never interested in true faith and honest intentions, only in belonging to and supporting the winning clique.

"The second brutal event was Bentze's love for Tsvetl, Feitl's wife. Bentze had left behind in Warsaw a wife and children, but now it was more expeditious for him to become close to Tsvetl. I saw them kiss and embrace while on the run. They were caressing each other like two old lovers. When she offered him some tidbit, he ate it from her hand. She seemed to have completely forgotten about Feitl, who was left kilometers behind. Laden as Bentze was with his own packs, he took Tsvetl's box and she paid him back with sausages and pretzels. It was all so obvious, and shamelessly true to the eternal laws of human conduct.

"We had come to a village—I don't remember its name—and there was no trace of war there. It's not clear to me to this day whether it was already Stalin's part of Poland or no-man's-land. Jews came out to meet us with bread, water, milk. There was no hotel in that village and the refugees went to sleep in the studyhouse or the poorhouse. Since Bentze and Tsvetl were two of the first to get there, they both found lodgings in the house of a local Stalinist. Some hours later I saw Feitl in the studyhouse lying on a bench, barefoot, with swollen feet full of blisters. He was so confused and broken that he did not recognize me, although we had met every day in the Writers' Club. I told him who I was, and he said, 'Zeinvel, I don't belong to this world anymore.'

"I was afraid that he might die then and there, but he finally managed to make it to Bialystok, and there the Stalinists held court, judging him. I was told that he had to confess all his sins against the masses and to call himself a Fascist, a Hitler spy, and an enemy of the people. As far as I know, he escaped from Bialystok to Wilno, and there, I think, he perished at the hands of the Nazis. I had my own troubles in Bialystok. I, too, had to run away, but this, as they say, is a chapter in itself.

"About what went on in Bialystok between 1939 and 1941, one could write a whole literature. For a short time the Warsaw Stalinists became powerful. They organized their own NKVD. They dug up old Yiddish newspapers and magazines, and began an inquisition of other Yiddish writers. A young man who had been a Marxist literary critic in Warsaw had become an expert in finding traces of counter-revolution, Fascism, Trotskyism, right deviation, left deviation in poems, stories, and plays. Someone had written a poem about spring and this critic managed to find in such innocent words as 'flowers' and 'butterflies' allusions to Mussolini, Léon Blum, Trotsky, and Norman Thomas. The birds were not just simple birds but the bands of Denikin and Makhno. The flowers were nothing but symbols for the counter-revolutionists Rykov, Kamenev, and Zinoviev, who had already been purged. Bentze was one of the judges. It wasn't long before the Stalinists began to denounce one another to the authorities from Soviet Russia. It all lasted until June 1941, when the Nazis marched into Bialystok and whoever managed to remain alive had to run again."

"What happened to Bentze?" I asked. "Is he still alive?".

"Alive?" Zeinvel cried out. "Not one of those people is alive. They were all liquidated sooner or later. In 1941 I had the good luck to reach Shanghai, but someone told me that when Bentze finally got to Soviet Russia and threw himself on the ground to kiss the earth of the socialistic land, a Red Army man clutched him by his collar and arrested him. He was sent somewhere to the north to a place where the strongest man could not last longer than one year. Hundreds of thousands such as

Bentze were exiled to a sure death, all in the name of a better morning and a beautiful future."

"What happened to Tsvetl?" I asked.

"What? In 1948 she managed to get to Israel. There she remarried, and then she died of cancer."

Zeinvel Markus flicked the ashes of his cigarette into a cup of cold coffee. He said, "This is what human beings are, this is their history, and I am afraid this is also their future. Meanwhile, let's have another cup of coffee."

Translated by the author and Lester Goran

The Missing Line

TOWARD EVENING, the large hall of the Yiddish Writers' Club in Warsaw became almost empty. At a table in a corner two unemployed proofreaders played chess. They seemed to play and doze simultaneously. Mina, the cat, had forgotten she was a literary cat written up in the newspapers and went out in the yard to hunt for a mouse or perhaps a bird. I was sitting at a table with the most important member of the club— Joshua Gottlieb, the main feuilletonist of *The Haint*. He was the president of the journalists' syndicate, a doctor of philosophy, a former student of such famous scholars as Hermann Cohen, Professor Bauch, Professor Messer Leon, Kuno Fischer. Dr. Gottlieb was tall, broad-shouldered, with a straight red neck and a potbelly. The setting sun threw a purple shine on his huge bald head. He smoked a long cigar and blew the smoke out through his nostrils. He would not have invited a beginner like myself to his table, but there was no one else available at this hour, and he liked to talk and tell stories.

Our conversation turned to the supernatural and Dr. Gottlieb was saying, "You young men are in a rush to explain everything according to your theories. For you it is theory first and facts last. If the facts don't match the theories, it is the fault of the facts. But a man of my age knows that events have a logic of their own. Above all, they are the product of causality. Your mystics feel insulted if things happen in what we call a natural way. But to me the greatest and most wonderful miracle is what Spinoza called the order of things. When I lose my glasses and then find them in a drawer which I thought I hadn't opened in two years, I know I must have put them there myself and that they were not hidden by your demons or imps. I also know that no matter how many incantations I might have recited to retrieve them, the eyeglasses would have stayed in the drawer forever. As you know, I am a great admirer of Kant, but to me causality is more than a category of pure reason. It is the very essence of creation. You may even call it the thing in itself."

"Who made causality?" I asked, just to say something.

"No one, and therein is its beauty. Let me tell you— about two years ago something happened to me which had all the earmarks of one of your miracles. I was absolutely convinced that no explanation of it was possible. Rationalist that I am, I said to myself, If this actually happened and it was not a dream, I will have to reappraise everything I learned from the first grade in Gymnasium to the universities of Bonn and Bern. But then I heard the explanation and it was as convincing and as simple as only the truth can be. As a matter of fact, I thought I would write a story about it myself. However, I don't want to compete with our literati. I guess you know that I don't have too high an opinion of fiction. It may sound like a sacrilege to you, but I find more human fallacies, more psychology, and even more entertainment in the daily press than in all your literary magazines. Does my cigar bother you?"

"Not at all."

"You certainly know—I don't need to tell you—that our typesetters on *The Haint* and in the Yiddish press generally make more errors than all the other typesetters in the whole world. Although they consider themselves ardent Yiddishists, they don't have the slightest respect for their language. I don't sleep nights because of these barbarians. Who was it who said that 99 percent of all writers die not from cancer or consumption but from misprints. Every week I read three proofs of my Friday feuilleton, but when they correct one mistake they immediately make another, and sometimes two, three, or four.

"About two years ago I happened to write an article about Kant, a *jubilieum* of a sort. When it comes to philosophic terms, our typesetters get especially rattled. Besides, the man who makes up the page layout has a tradition of losing at least one line from my feuilleton every time, and I often find it in another article, sometimes even in the news. On that day I quoted a phrase which offered a perfect target for misprints: *the tran-*

scendental unity of the apperception. I knew our type-setters would make mincemeat out of it, but I had to use it. I read the proofs three times as usual, and miraculously the words came out correctly every time. But I uttered a little prayer for the future, just in case. That night I went to sleep as hopeful as a writer in Yiddish can afford to be.

"The papers are brought to me every morning about eight o'clock, and Friday is always my crisis day of the week. At first everything seemed quite smooth and I hoped against hope that this time I would be spared. But no, the line with the words 'the transcendental unity of the apperception' was missing. The whole article became senseless.

"Of course I was angry and cursed all the Yiddish typesetters with the vilest oaths. After an hour of utter resentment and extreme anti-Yiddishism, I began a search for the line in the other articles and news items of our Friday issue. But this time it seemed to have been lost altogether. Somehow this was a disappointment to me. What burned me up more than anything else is that readers, even my friends in the Writers' Club, complimented me and seemed not to have noticed the missing line. I've promised myself a million times not to read *The Haint* on Friday, but you know, there is an element of masochism in each of us. In my imagination I took revenge on the typesetters, the editors, the proof-readers by shooting them, beating them, and making them memorize all my feuilletons since the year 1910.

"After a while, I decided I had suffered enough and began to read *The Moment*, our rival newspaper, to see what their feuilletonist, Mr. Helfman, had written that Friday. Of course I knew beforehand that his piece could not be anything but bad. In all twenty years of our competition, I've never read anything good by this scribbler. I don't know how you feel about him, but to me he is an abomination.

"That Friday, his concoction seemed worse than ever, so I gave up in the middle and began to read the news. I turned to an item with the title 'A Man a Beast,' the story of a janitor who came home from the tavern at night and raped his daughter. Suddenly the most impossible, unbelievable, preposterous thing happened —my missing line was right before my eyes! I knew that it must be a hallucination. However, hallucinations last no longer than a split second. Here the words lingered in black type before me: *the transcendental unity of the apperception* . . . I closed my eyes, certain that when I opened them again the mirage would have vanished, but when I did there it was—the unthinkable, the ridiculous, the absurd.

"I admit that even while disbelieving in what you call the supernatural, I often toyed with the idea that one day a phenomenon might occur which would force me to lose faith in logic and reality. But that a metal line would fly from the *Haint* composing room at 8 Chlodna Street to the *Moment* composing room at 38 Nelewski —this I certainly did not expect. My son came into the room, and I must have looked as if I had seen a ghost, because he said to me, 'Papa, what's the matter?' I don't know why, but I said to him, 'Please, go down and buy me a copy of *The Moment*.' 'But you are reading

The Moment right now,' my boy said. I told him that I must see another copy. The boy looked at me as if to say, 'The old man is meshugga altogether,' but he went down and bought another copy.

"Sure enough, my line was there on the same page in the same item: 'He came home from the tavern and saw his daughter in bed and *the transcendental unity of the apperception . . .*' I was so baffled and distressed that I began to laugh. To be completely on the safe side, I asked my boy to read the whole item out loud. Again he gave me that look which meant 'My father is not all there,' but he read it slowly. When he came to the transposed line, he smiled and asked, 'Is this why you wanted me to buy another copy?' I didn't answer. I knew that no hallucination has ever been shared by two people."

"There are cases of collective hallucinations," I said.

"Anyhow, that Friday and Saturday I couldn't sleep and could barely eat. I decided to go on Sunday morning to speak to the manager of our printing department, my old friend, Mr. Gavza. If there is a man who cannot be fooled by abracadabra and hocus-pocus, it is he. I wanted to see the expression on his face when he saw what I saw. On the way to *The Haint* I decided it would be a good thing to find the manuscript of my feuilleton, assuming it wasn't thrown out. I asked if the copy of my article was still around, and lo and behold, they found it, and the words were there as I remembered them. I was eager to find the solution to this riddle, but I didn't want the solution to be based on some silly blunder, ludicrous misunderstanding, or lapse of memory. With my manuscript in one hand and *The Moment* in the other, I went to see Mr. Gavza. I showed him my manuscript and said, 'Please, read this paragraph.' Before I even finished my sentence he said, 'I know, I know, a line was missing in your feuilleton about Kant. I guess you want to publish a correction. Believe me, no one ever reads them.' 'No, I don't want to publish any corrections,' I said. 'What else brings you here on Sunday morning?' Gavza asked.

"I showed him the Friday *Moment* with the news item and said, 'Now read this.' Gavza shrugged, began to read, and never before have I seen an expression like that on Gavza's quiet face. He gaped at the news item, at my manuscript, at me, at the paper, again at me, and said, 'Am I seeing things? This is your missing line!'

" 'Yes, my friend,' I said. 'My missing line has jumped from *The Haint* to *The Moment* a dozen streets away, over all the buildings, all the rooftops, and settled down right into their printing room, into this item. Is it possible that demons did the job? If you can explain this . . .'

" 'Really, I cannot believe it,' Gavza said. 'This must be some trick, some kind of practical joke. Maybe someone glued in the line. Let me see it again.'

" 'No trick and no glue,' I said. 'This line fell out of my article and appeared in *The Moment* last Friday. I have another copy of *The Moment* in my pocket.'

" 'My God, how could this have happened?' Gavza asked. Again and again he compared my manuscript with the line in *The Moment*. Then I heard him say, 'If this can happen, anything can happen. Maybe demons really did steal your line from *The Haint* and carry it to *The Moment*.'

"For a long while we stood looking at each other with the painful feeling of two adults who realize that their world has turned to chaos, with logic gone and so-called reality totally bankrupt. Then Gavza burst out laughing. 'No, it wasn't the demons, not even the angels. I think I know what happened,' he exclaimed.

" 'Tell me quickly before I burst,' I said.

"And this was his explanation. The Jewish National Fund often publishes an appeal in both *The Haint* and *The Moment*. Sometimes they make changes to adjust the appeal for the readers of the respective newspapers. Then they don't make a matrix but carry the whole metal page by car from one newspaper to the other for adjustments. By error, my line must have been put into the metal page of the appeal. It was carried over to *The Moment* and there someone noticed the mistake, took out the line from the appeal page, and it promptly got stuck into this news item. 'The chances that such a thing should happen are not as small as one may think, considering our sort of typesetters and proofreaders,' Gavza said. 'They are the worst bunglers. No, let's not put the blame on the poor demons. No demon is as ignorant and as careless as our printers and printer's devils.'

"We had a great laugh, and in honor of that historic solution, we went and had coffee and cake. We spoke about old times and the countless absurdities published in the Yiddish press, God bless it. Especially strange were the misprints listed in the back of Yiddish books, such as: On page 69 it is printed, 'She went to see her mother in Bialystok' —It should read: 'He had a long gray beard.' Or: On page 87 it is written, 'He had a very strong appetite.' —It should have said, 'He went to see his former wife in Vilna.' On page 379, 'They took the train to Lublin.' —It should have been, 'The chicken was not kosher.' How a typesetter can make mistakes of this kind will always be a riddle to me. Another article was written about bacteria, 'which are so small that they can be seen only with the help of a telescope.' "

Dr. Gottlieb paused, trying to revive his extinguished cigar, sucking at it violently. Then he said, "My young friend, I tell you all this just to prove to you that one should not be in a rush to decide that Mother Nature has given up her eternal laws. As far as I'm concerned, the goblins and sprites have not taken over, and the laws of nature are still valid, whether I like them or not. And when I have to convey a message to my old wife, or to my not-much-younger girlfriend, I still use the telephone, not telepathy."

Translated by the author

The Hotel

WHEN ISRAEL Danziger retired to Miami Beach it seemed to him as if he were retiring to the other world. At the age of fifty-six he had been compelled to abandon everything he had known: the factory in New York, his houses, the office, his children, his relatives, and his friends. Hilda, his wife, bought a house with a garden on the banks of Indian Creek. It had comfortable rooms on the ground floor, a patio, a swimming pool, palms, flower beds, a gazebo, and special chairs designed to put little strain on the heart. The creek stank a bit, but there was a cool breeze from the ocean just across the street.

The water was green and glassy, like a stage decoration at the opera, with white ships skimming over its surface. Seagulls squeaked shrilly above and swooped down to catch fish. On the white sands lay half-naked women. Israel Danziger did not need binoculars to view them; he could see them behind his sunglasses. He could even hear their gabble and laughter.

He had no worries of being forgotten. They would all come down from New York in the winter to visit him—his sons, his daughters, and their in-laws. Hilda was already concerned about not having enough bedrooms and linen, and also that Israel might have too much excitement with all the visitors from the city. His doctor had prescribed complete rest.

It was September now, and Miami Beach was deserted. The hotels closed their doors, posting signs that they would reopen in December or January. In the cafeterias downtown, which only yesterday had swarmed with people, chairs were piled atop bare tables, the lights extinguished, and business at a standstill. The sun blazed, but the newspapers were full of warnings of a hurricane from some far-off island, admonishing their readers to prepare candles, water, and storm windows, although it was far from certain whether the hurricane would touch Miami. It might bypass Florida entirely and push out into the Atlantic.

The newspapers were bulky and boring. The same news items which stirred the senses in New York seemed dull and meaningless here. The radio programs were vacuous and television was idiotic. Even books by well-known writers seemed flat.

Israel still had an appetite, but Hilda carefully doled out his rations. Everything he liked was forbidden—full of cholesterol—butter, eggs, milk, coffee with cream, a piece of fat meat. Instead she filled him up with cottage cheese, salads, mangoes, and orange juice, and even this was measured out to him by the ounce lest, heaven forbid, he might swallow a few extra calories.

Israel Danziger lay on a deck chair, clad only in swimming trunks and beach sandals. A fig tree cast its shadow over him; yet he still covered his bald pate with a straw cap. Without clothes, Israel Danziger wasn't Israel Danziger at all; he was just a little man, a bundle of skin and bones, with a single tuft of hair on his chest, protruding ribs, knobby knees, and arms like sticks. Despite all the suntan lotion he had smeared on himself, his skin was covered with red blotches. Too much sun had inflamed his eyes.

He got up and immersed himself in the swimming pool, splashed around for a few minutes, and then climbed out again. He couldn't swim; all he did was dip himself, as if in a *mikvah*. Some weeks ago he had actually begun to read a book, but he couldn't finish it. Every day he read the Yiddish newspaper from beginning to end, including the advertisements.

He carried with him a pad and pencil, and from time to time he would estimate how much he was worth. He added up the profits from his apartment houses in New York and the dividends earned by his stocks and bonds. And each time the result was the same. Even if he was to live to be a hundred, Israel Danziger would still have more than enough, and there'd even be plenty for his heirs. Yet he could never really believe it. How and when did he amass such a fortune? And what would he do during all the years he still was destined to live: sit in the deck chair and gaze up at the sky?

Israel Danziger wanted to smoke, but the doctor allowed him only two cigars a day, and even that might be harmful. To dull his appetite for tobacco and for food, Israel chewed unsweetened gum. He bent down, plucked a blade of grass, and studied it. Then his eyes wandered to an orange tree nearby. He wondered what he would have thought if someone in Parciewe, his hometown in Poland, had told him that one day he would own a house in America, with citrus and coconut trees on the shores of the Atlantic Ocean in a land of eternal summer. Now he had all this, but what was it worth?

Suddenly Israel Danziger tensed. He thought he heard the telephone ringing inside. A long-distance call from New York, perhaps? He got up to answer it, and realized it was just a cricket which made a noise like a bell. No one ever called him here. Who would call him? When a man liquidates his business, he's like a corpse.

Israel Danziger looked around again. The sky was pale blue, without even a cloud-puff. A single bird flew high above him. Where was it flying? The women who earlier had lain in the sand were now in the ocean. Although the sea was as smooth as a lake, they jumped up and down as if there were waves. They were fat, ugly, and broad-shouldered. There was about them a selfishness that sickens the souls of men. And for such parasites men worked, weakened their hearts, and died before their times?

Israel had also driven himself beyond his strength. The doctors had warned him. Israel spat on the ground. Hilda was supposed to be a faithful wife, but just let him close his eyes and she'd have another husband within a year, and this time she'd pick a taller man . . .

But what was he to do? Build a synagogue where no one comes to pray? Have a Torah inscribed that nobody would read? Give away money to a kibbutz and help the atheists live in free love? You couldn't even give money to charity these days. For whatever purpose you gave, the money was eaten up by secretaries, fund-raisers, and politicians. By the time it was supposed to reach the needy, there was nothing left.

In the same notebook that Israel Danziger used to total up his income lay several letters which he had received only that morning. One from a yeshiva in Brooklyn, another from a Yiddish poet who was preparing to publish his work, a third from a home for the aged which wanted to build a new wing. The letters all sang the same refrain—send us a check. But what good would come of a few additional students at the yeshiva in Williamsburg? Who needed the poet's new verse? And why build a new wing? So that the president could arrange a banquet and take the cream off the milk? Perhaps the president was a builder himself, or else he had a son-in-law who was an architect. I know that bunch, Israel Danziger grumbled to himself. They can't bluff me.

Israel Danziger couldn't remain seated any longer. He was engulfed by an emptiness as painful as any heart attack. The force that keeps men alive was draining from him and he knew without a doubt that he was only one step away from death, from madness. He had to do something immediately. He ran inside to his bedroom, flung open the doors of his closet, put on pants, a pair of socks, a shirt, a pair of shoes, then took up his cane and went out. His car was waiting in the garage, but he didn't want to drive a car and speed without purpose over the highway. Hilda was out shopping for groceries; the house would be empty, but no one stole things here. And what did it matter if someone did try to break in? Besides, Joe the gardener was out tending the lawns, sprinkling water from a hose onto the bluish grass that had been brought here in sheets and now was spread over the sand like a carpet. Even the grass here has no roots, Israel Danziger thought. He envied Joe. At least that black man was doing something. He had a family somewhere near Miami.

What Israel Danziger was living through now was not mere boredom; it was panic. He had to act or perish. Maybe go to his broker and see how his stocks were getting along? But he'd already been there that morning for an hour. If he should take to going there twice a day, he would become a nuisance. Besides, it was now twenty minutes to three. By the time he got there, they'd be closed.

The bus station was just across the street, and a bus was pulling up. Israel Danziger ran across the road, and this very act was like a drop of medicine. He climbed on the bus and threw in the coin. He'd go to Paprov's cafeteria. There he'd buy the afternoon paper, an exact duplicate of the morning paper, drink a cup of coffee, eat a piece of cake, smoke a cigar, and, who knows, perhaps he would meet someone he knew.

The bus was half empty. The passengers all sat on the shaded side and fanned themselves, some with fans, others with folded newspapers, and still others with the flaps of pocketbooks. Only one passenger sat on the side where the sun burned, a man who was beyond caring about heat. He looked unkempt, unshaven, and dirty. Must be a drunk, Israel Danziger thought, and for the first time he understood drunkenness. He'd take a shot of whiskey, too, if he were allowed. Anything is better than this hollowness.

A passenger got off and Israel Danziger took his seat. A hot wind blew in through the open window. It tasted of the ocean, of half-melted asphalt and gasoline. Israel Danziger sat quietly. But suddenly perspiration broke out over all his body and his fresh shirt was soaked in a second. He grew more cheerful. He had reached the point where even a bus ride was an adventure.

On Lincoln Road were stores, shop windows, restaurants, banks. Newsboys were hawking papers. It was a little like a real city, almost like New York. Beneath one of the storefront awnings, Israel Danziger saw a poster advertising a big sale. The entire stock was to be sold. To Israel Danziger, Lincoln Road seemed like an oasis in the wilderness. He found himself worrying about the owners of the stores. How long would they hold out if they never saw a customer? He felt impelled to buy something, anything, to help business. It's a good deed, he told himself, better than giving to shnorrers.

The bus stopped, and Israel Danziger got off and entered the cafeteria. The revolving door, the air-conditioned chill, the bright lights burning in the middle of the day, the hubbub of customers, the clatter of dishes, the long steam tables laden with food and drink, the cashier ringing the cash register, the smell of tobacco— all this revived the spirit of Israel Danziger. He shook off his melancholy, his hypochondria and thoughts of death. With his right hand he grabbed a tray; his left hand he stuck into his rear pocket, where he had some bills and small change. He remembered his doctor's warnings, but a greater power—a power which makes the final decision—told him to go ahead. He bought a chopped-herring sandwich, a tall glass of iced coffee, and a piece of cheese cake. He lit a long cigar. He was Israel Danziger again, a living person, a businessman.

At another table, across from Israel Danziger, sat a little man, no taller than Danziger but stocky, broad-shouldered, with a large head and a fat neck. He wore an expensive Panama hat (at least fifty dollars, Danziger figured), and a pink, short-sleeved shirt. On one of his fingers, plump as a sausage, a diamond glittered. He was puffing a cigar and leafing through a Yiddish newspaper, breaking off pieces from an egg pretzel. He removed his hat, and his bald head shone round and smooth. There was something childlike about his round-ness, his fatness, and his puckered lips. He was not smoking his cigar; he was only sucking at it, and Israel Danziger wondered who he was. Certainly he was not a native. Perhaps a New Yorker? But what was he doing here in September, unless he suffered from hay fever? And, since he was reading a Yiddish paper, Israel

Danziger knew he was one of the family. He wanted to get to know the man. For a while he hesitated; it wasn't like him to approach strangers. But here in Miami you can die of boredom if you're too reserved. He got up from his chair, took the plate with the cheese cake and the coffee, and moved over to the other man's table.

"Anything new in the paper?"

The man removed the cigar from his mouth. "What should be new? Nothing. Not a thing."

"In the old days there were writers, today scribblers," said Israel Danziger, just to say something.

"It's five cents wasted."

"Well, what else can you do in Miami? It helps kill time."

"What are you doing here in this heat?"

"And what are you doing here?"

"It's my heart . . . I'm sitting around here six months already. The doctor exiled me here . . . I had to retire . . ."

"So—then we're brothers!" Israel Danziger exclaimed. "I have a heart, too, a bad heart that gives me trouble. I got rid of everything in New York, and my good wife bought me a house with fig trees, like in Palestine in the old days. I sit around and go crazy."

"Where is the house?"

Danziger told him.

"I pass it every day. I think I even saw you there once. What did you do before?"

Danziger told him.

"I myself have been in real estate for over thirty-five years," the other man said.

The two men fell into a conversation. The little man in the Panama hat said his name was Morris Sapirstone. He had an apartment on Euclid Avenue. Israel Danziger got up and bought two cups of coffee and two more egg pretzels. Then he offered him one of his cigars, and Sapirstone gave him one of his brand. After fifteen minutes they were talking as if they had known each other for years.

They had moved in the same circles in New York; both came from Poland. Sapirstone took out a wallet of alligator leather and showed Israel Danziger photographs of his wife, two daughters, two sons-in-law— one a doctor, one a lawyer—and several grandchildren. One granddaughter looked like a copy of Sapirstone. The woman was fat, like a Sabbath stew pot. Compared to her, his Hilda was a beauty. Danziger wondered how a man could live with such an ugly woman. On the other hand, he reflected, with one of her kind, you wouldn't be as lonesome as he was with Hilda. A woman like that would always have a swarm of chattering biddies around her.

Israel Danziger had never been pious, but since his heart attack and his retirement to Miami Beach he had begun to think in religious terms. Now he beheld the finger of God in his coming together with Morris Sapirstone.

"Do you play chess?" he asked.

"Chess, no. But I do play pinochle."

"Is there anybody to play with?"

"I find them."

"You're a smart man. I can't find anybody. I sit around all day long and don't see a soul."

"Why did you settle so far uptown?"

In the course of their talk Morris Sapirstone mentioned that there was a hotel for sale. It was almost a new hotel, all the way uptown. The owners had gone bankrupt, and the bank was ready to sell it for a song. All you needed was a quarter of a million in cash. Israel Danziger was far from ready for a business proposition, but he listened eagerly. Talk of money, credit, banks, and mortgages cheered him up. It was proof, somehow, that the world had not yet come to an end. Israel Danziger knew nothing at all about hotels, but he picked up bits of information from Morris Sapirstone's story. The owners of the hotel had failed because they had sought a fancy clientele and made their rates too high. The rich people had stopped coming to Miami Beach. You had to attract the middle class. One good winter season and your investment would be covered. A new element was coming to Miami—the Latin Americans who chose Florida during their summers to "cool off." Israel Danziger groped in his shirt pocket for a pencil stub. While Morris went on talking, Israel wrote figures in the margin of his newspaper with great speed. At the same time, he plied Sapirstone with questions. How many rooms in the hotel? How much can one room bring in? What about taxes? Mortgages? Personnel costs? For

Israel, it was no more than a pastime, a reminder that once he, too, had been in business. He scratched his left temple with the point of the pencil.

"And what do you do if you have a bad season?"

"You have to see to it that it's good."

"How?"

"You have to advertise properly. Even in the Yiddish newspapers."

"Do they have a hall for conventions?"

An hour had passed and Israel Danziger did not know where it had gone. He clenched his cigar between his lips and turned it busily around in his mouth. New strength welled up inside him. His heart, which in recent months had alternately fluttered and hesitated, now worked as if he were a healthy man. Morris Sapirstone took a small box from his coat pocket, picked out a pill, and swallowed it with a drink of water.

"You had an attack, eh?"

"Two."

"For whom do I need a hotel? For my wife's second husband?"

Morris Sapirstone did not answer.

"How can I get to look at the hotel?" Israel Danziger asked after a while.

"Come with me."

"Do you have a car here?"

"The red Cadillac across the street."

"Ah, a nice Cadillac you got."

The two men left the cafeteria. Israel Danziger noticed that Sapirstone was using a cane. Water in his legs, he thought. An invalid and he's hunting for hotels . . . Sapirstone settled behind the steering wheel and started the engine. He gave a whack to the car behind him, but he didn't even turn around. Soon he was racing along. One hand expertly grasped the steering wheel; with the other, he worked a cigarette lighter. With a cigar clamped in his teeth, he mumbled on.

"There's no charge for looking."

"No."

"If my wife hears about this, she'll give me plenty of trouble. Before you know it, she'll tell the doctor and then they'll both eat me up alive."

"They told you to rest, eh?"

"And if they told me? One must rest *here*, in the head. But my mind doesn't rest. I lie awake at night and think about all kinds of nothings. And when you're up you get hungry. My wife went to a locksmith to find out whether she can put a lock on the refrigerator . . . All these diets make you more sick than well. How did people live in the old days? In my time there were no diets. My grandfather, he should rest in peace, used to eat up a whole plateful of onions and chicken fat as an appetizer. Then he got busy on the soup with drops of fat floating on top. Next he had a fat piece of meat. And he finished up with a shmaltz cake. Where was cholesterol then? My grandfather lived to be eighty-seven, and he died because he fell on the ice one winter. Let me tell you: someday they'll find out that cholesterol is healthy. They'll be taking cholesterol tablets just as they take vitamin pills today."

"I wish you were right."

"A man is like a Hanukkah dreidel. It gets a turn, and then it spins on by itself until it drops."

"On a smooth table, it'll spin longer."

"There aren't any smooth tables."

The car stopped. "Well, that's the hotel."

Israel Danziger took one look and saw everything in a moment. If it was true that you only had to lay down a quarter of a million, the hotel was a fantastic bargain. Everything was new. It must have cost a fortune to build. Of course it was located a little too far uptown, but the center was moving uptown now. Once, the Gentiles ran away from the Jews. Now the Jews were running away from the Jews. Across the street there was already a kosher meat market. Israel Danziger rubbed his forehead. He would have to put in a hundred and twenty-five thousand dollars as his share. He could borrow that much from the bank, giving his stocks as security. He might even be able to scrape together the cash without a loan. But should he really get involved in such headaches? It would be suicide, sheer suicide. What would Hilda say? And Dr. Cohen? They'd all be at me—Hilda, the boys, the girls, their husbands. That in itself could lead to a second attack . . .

Israel Danziger closed his eyes and for a while remained enveloped in his own darkness. Like a fortune-teller, he tried to project himself into the future and foresee what fate had in store for him. His mind became blank, dark, overcome with the numbness of sleep. He even heard himself snore. All his affairs, his entire life, hung in the balance this second. He was waiting for a command from within, a voice from his own depths

. . . Better to die than to go on living like this, he mumbled finally.

"What's the matter, Mr. Danziger, did you fall asleep?" he heard Sapirstone ask.

"Eh? No."

"So come in. Let's take a look at what's going on in here."

And the two little men climbed the steps to the fourteen-story hotel.

Translated by the author

Dazzled

THE TALK turned to the subject of maids, and Aunt Genendel was saying, "Maids are not something to belittle—they can create plenty of trouble. An entire regiment of Russian soldiers was once stationed in our town, which was close to the Austrian border. There was some conflict between Russia and Austria, and the military expected a war to break out. Or perhaps the Czar anticipated a new uprising by the Poles. These Russian soldiers were under the command of a colonel and some other officers. There were barracks for the soldiers and stables for the horses. Gendarmes rode through the streets on horseback with rifles slung over their backs and swords hanging at their sides. They spread fear among the Jews. But, on the other hand, they patronized the Jewish stores, and the owners profited.

"One day we heard that a highly important nobleman

named Orlov was coming from St. Petersburg—a distant member of the Czar's family, a duke. The news created excitement and confusion among the Russian officials, because a man of such high rank was almost never sent to a village as remote as ours. The quartermasters were especially concerned, because they had all taken bribes and submitted false accounts to their superiors. As a rule, the soldiers were given tasteless food, and their uniforms were not of the best quality, either. It was rumored that those who baked the bread kneaded the dough with their bare feet. The colonel immediately ordered that the soldiers be given better food and provided with decent clothing. The officers drilled the men with more rigor and warned them to say they were satisfied if the dignitary made inquiries. Instructions were given for the kitchens and kettles to be scrubbed and for the outhouses to be cleaned. Everyone had to shine his boots. A banquet was prepared for the duke, and the orchestra polished its instruments and rehearsed daily.

"Soon it was revealed that the great man was not coming for an inspection but was being exiled to our region as a punishment. He had challenged a high-ranking person to a duel and had killed him. Since putting one of the Czar's family in prison would create a scandal, they sent him to Poland for a few years.

"He arrived in an old coach drawn by two skinny horses and drove up to Lippe Reznik's inn instead of going to the quarters assigned to him. The duke looked shabby, worn-out, tired. He was short, with a little gray beard, and although he had the title of major general he was dressed like a civilian. He must have lost all his prestige in St. Petersburg. Without stripes, epaulets, and medals, the greatest lord is not more than flesh and blood. After seeing the duke, the colonel canceled his orders, and the soldiers were again given nothing but kasha and cabbage. They stopped shining their boots three times a day. The orchestra fell silent. Still, the colonel and his underlings came to pay the duke a visit at Lippe Reznik's inn. I wasn't there, but Lippe said that the duke received his guests impatiently and did not even offer them a seat. When the colonel inquired as to what His Highness needed, he answered that he needed absolutely nothing and that all he wanted was to be left in peace.

"For some reason, the duke was friendly to the Jews. One of them, a real-estate broker, suggested he buy an old wood house, and the duke took it immediately. The broker also offered him a maid. Antosha was her name —the widow of a soldier who died in the war with the Turks. She did the wash for Jewish homes and lived alone in a half-ruined hut. The truth was that she was not even fit to be a washerwoman. She once did our laundry, and everything came out so dirty that my mother had to have it redone. She couldn't iron, bleach, or prepare the wash for the mangle. An ignorant, unfortunate creature she was, but she happened to have a pretty little face for a woman of her age—blue eyes, blond hair, a chiseled nose. If I am not mistaken, she was a bastard sired by some Polish landowner. She had one good quality: she was not greedy for money. No matter

what she was paid, she thanked the mistress profusely
and kissed her hand. When the broker told him about
Antosha, the duke asked to see her. Antosha had one
dress, which she wore to church on Sundays, and one
pair of shoes, which she usually carried in her hands.
In these clothes, she was brought to the duke. He took
one look and agreed to have her. He promised to pay
her a wage excessive for a servant of such low caliber.
He was quick in everything he did. Each day he walked
on Lublin Street and strode so briskly that he overtook
all the passersby. There was an Orthodox church near
the barracks, but he never attended the services, even
on Easter or on the Russian New Year. He got a reputation as a heretic and a madman. In the beginning, he
used to receive a lot of mail, but he answered no one,
and after a while the mailman brought him only one
letter a month—the money order for his pension.

"There was a grocery store close to the duke's house.
The owner, Mendel, and his wife, Baila Gitl, had become quite familiar with the duke. They provided him
with everything he needed—even things that could not
ordinarily be found in a grocery store, such as ink,
steel pens, writing paper, wine, vodka, tobacco. Baila
Gitl noticed that Antosha was ordering more food than
two people could eat. On one trip, she would buy three
pounds of butter and ten dozen eggs. She was keeping
food so long that it became rotten and had to be thrown
out. The duke complained to Baila Gitl that Antosha
attracted mice and vermin into the house. Baila Gitl ad-
vised him to get rid of her and find a maid with more
sense, but the duke said, 'I cannot do this to her. She

might be jealous.' Apparently, he was living with this simpleton. I shouldn't sin with my words, but a man doesn't need a woman with intelligence. All he needs, you should excuse me, is a piece of flesh."

"Don't say this, Genendel!" Chaya Riva, a neighbor, cried out. "Not all men are the same."

"Huh? They are all the same," Genendel said. "There was a rabbi in Lublin who was called the Iron Head. He was a great scholar and learned in the Torah, but his wife, the rebbetzin, could not even read the prayer book. On the Sabbath and on holidays, a woman had to recite the prayers to her. All the rebbetzin could do was say 'Amen.'"

"Why didn't her husband teach her?" Chaya Riva asked.

"*Nu*, who knows? Now the real story begins. The duke tried to explain to Antosha that some food cannot be kept for weeks and months. But the peasant could not grasp this. She would sweep up the rubbish and leave it lying for days in the corner where the broom stood. Baila Gitl often saw the duke himself taking the garbage out to the rubbish pit. This Antosha was like Yussel in the Golem story. If they told him to bring water from the well, he brought so much water that it flooded the entire house. Antosha couldn't cook, either. She oversalted a dish or she forgot to salt it altogether. It got to the point where the duke would put on an apron and cook his own meal. How can a man of such high birth fall so low? He was a scholar, always reading books or writing. He was so absorbed in his own thoughts he would sometimes let the milk boil over and the meat burn.

"Baila Gitl lived in an apartment over the store, and from there she could see all the goings-on with her own eyes. She tried to teach Antosha to keep house, but it was in vain. Antosha would only say, 'Yes, yes, yes, dear mistress, I will do everything you teach me.' She wept and kissed Baila Gitl's hand, but she could never learn a thing."

"A blockhead, huh?" Chaya Riva asked.

"Silly and stubborn," Genendel answered.

"She probably gave him a lot of pleasure in bed," Chaya Riva said.

Aunt Genendel seemed embarrassed. "What can a female do more than she does? One way or another, things became worse with time. The duke began to complain to Baila Gitl that he suffered stomach pains from Antosha's cooking. A few times, Baila Gitl brought him a dish of grits or chicken broth and he ate in silence. Once, he said to her, 'On account of a foolish suspicion, I killed a friend. From sorrow and shame my wife passed away. I sinned, and here I must pay for my sin.' Later, when Baila Gitl recounted this story to her friends, she would say, 'A Gentile penitent—who has ever heard of such a thing?'

"Now listen to this. Antosha had never learned to use matches. She would light a match, forget to blow it out, then throw it right on the floor or into the garbage bucket. A few times the rubbish went up in flames.

This could have started a terrible fire, but the duke happened to notice and extinguished the flames. Many times he warned Antosha that she must blow out a match before she threw it away, but each time she forgot anew. In the half-ruined hut where Antosha had lived before, there was no wooden floor, just earth, and nothing could catch fire there.

"The duke had brought books and various papers from Russia. It seemed that he was writing a book. In the evening he wrote by a kerosene lamp with a green shade. Once, late at night, when the duke was sitting and writing, he heard a scream, and when he looked up he saw that the kitchen was on fire. It was too late to try to put the flames out with a pail of water, because the entire building was burning. Antosha had thrown a lit match into the refuse and then had taken a nap. When she awoke, she saw the blaze and apparently threw herself over the flames, and her dress caught fire. The duke rushed into the kitchen, lifted Antosha in his arms, and ran outside with her. His housecoat was also ablaze. Both of them would have burned to a crisp, but there was a drainage ditch nearby, and it had rained earlier. The duke threw Antosha and himself into the ditch. Thus, Antosha remained alive, but without hair and practically without a face. The duke was also burned, but not as severely as she. He had enough strength to call for help, and Baila Gitl heard his cry and woke her husband. Had the fire gone on a bit longer, Baila Gitl's house and the store and possibly the entire street would have gone up in smoke. By the time

the firemen were awakened and had come with their
old hoses and half-filled barrels of water, nothing was
left of the duke's property but a heap of ashes."

Aunt Genendel nodded and blew her nose. She wiped
her brass-rimmed glasses with her handkerchief and
went on. "The colonel had long since left town. His
regiment had been transferred even closer to the Austrian border, near the river San. But the remaining
soldiers had a sort of makeshift hospital, which consisted of one room with three beds, and there the duke
took Antosha—a bundle of burned flesh, a sack of bones.
She was neither alive nor dead. The military doctor, an
old drunk, suggested they smear her with fat, but as
they applied the grease her skin peeled off like an
onion's. She had become as black as pitch, almost a
skeleton. But as long as one breathes one is still alive.
In comparison with her, the duke got off lightly, but not
entirely. His beard was singed and would never grow
back. Blisters covered his hands and forehead. Antosha
was completely at fault, but still he worried only about
her recovery. He pleaded with the doctor to save her.
The doctor said openly, 'She will not last long.' Antosha
could not speak but squeaked like a mouse. She also
became blind.

"Meanwhile, the news of this calamity reached St.
Petersburg, and it created a commotion. People there
had already forgotten about the exiled duke, but when
they heard that he lay sick in some remote village in
Poland and was left without a shirt on his back it

aroused compassion among his former friends. The news reached the Czar (not the present Czar but his father), and he decreed that the duke should be brought back to Russia. The Czar sent a doctor and a male nurse, and asked that the governor of Lublin be notified. The event was written about in the newspapers. Reporters came and asked the townspeople a lot of questions: How did the duke live? With whom did he have dealings? This, that. The local Russians were hostile to the duke, because he had avoided them. The Poles certainly didn't have a good word to say about a Russian. But the Jews praised him. He had given charity to the poor and to the sick in the poorhouse. An entire group of officials arrived in town. The Czar had demanded that the exiled duke be sent home in style. They all knew quite well that he had a common mistress, a Polish maid who now wrangled with death, but, of course, they didn't give a hoot about her. They prepared a coach for him with eight horses. The entourage was to travel to Lublin and from there in a special railway car to St. Petersburg. But the Russians had, as they say, made their plans without the boss. The duke insisted that he could not leave without Antosha."

"He was still in love with her, huh?" Chaya Riva asked.

"Dazzled," Aunt Genendel answered.

"How can an important man care about a creature like her?" another neighbor asked.

"People in love are half insane," Genendel replied.

"What happened then?" Chaya Riva asked.

Aunt Genendel rubbed her forehead. "I forget where I was—you shouldn't have interrupted me. Yes, the officials were indignant. How could they bring her to St. Petersburg? Besides, she was at the threshold of death. They waited for her to die, but many days passed and she lived. Woe to such a life! After many arguments, the officials lost their patience. They sent a telegram to St. Petersburg saying that the defiant duke was no longer in his right mind, and the answer came back that they should leave him where he was.

"Now listen to this. The morning after the Russians left, the duke went to the Orthodox priest and asked him to marry him and Antosha. The priest couldn't believe his ears. 'Marry you? She is as good as a corpse!' he cried out. And the duke answered, 'According to the law, one is allowed to marry a person as long as he or she breathes.'

"I will not keep you much longer. The duke bought a wedding gown for Antosha and dragged the sick woman out of bed. Two soldiers carried her on a stretcher to the Orthodox church, the *tserkov*. The entire town—Jews and Gentiles both—came to stare at the bizarre wedding. People expected the bride to expire before the ceremony began, but somehow she lived. I doubt whether she knew what they were doing to her. The Polish priest contended that she was Catholic, not Orthodox, and that the Russian didn't have the right to marry her in their ritual. But the Russians were in power, not the Poles. The bells rang, the organ played, a Russian choir sang, and the groom stood there in a borrowed uniform and with a seared-off beard. Only his sword and a medal had been saved from the fire.

"Three days after the wedding, Antosha finally gave up her soul. It was a victory for the Poles that she was buried in the Polish cemetery, not in the Russian one. A few months later, the duke caught pneumonia and he, too, passed on. In his will he asked to be buried next to Antosha, but the authorities would not permit this. A dispatch came from St. Petersburg, ordering that the duke be buried with military honors. The governor of Lublin came to the funeral, the orchestra played, an old cannon was found and salutes were fired. You will not believe me, but the Jews had recited Psalms when the duke was sick. The rabbi said that in his way the duke was like a saint."

Aunt Genendel blew her nose, and wiped a tear with the edge of her shawl. "Why do I tell you all this? To show that a maid is not something to brush off with a wave of the hand. In olden times, maids were concubines to their masters. Even today, when a man is left without a wife the maid often acts as the wife. I know a story about a rabbi who fell in love with his maid and married her when he became a widower—he an old man of seventy with a white beard and she a wench of fourteen, the daughter of a water carrier."

"The town allowed this?" Chaya Riva asked.

"The elders were so furious that they exiled both of them one Friday on a cart drawn by oxen," Genendel said.

"Why by oxen?" Chaya Riva asked.

Aunt Genendel thought for a while. "Because oxen move slowly, and before this lovesick pair could reach an inhabited place the sun would have set and they would have to make the Sabbath in the middle of the road."

Translated by Deborah Menashe

Sabbath in Gehenna

ON THE Sabbath, as is known, the fires do not burn in Gehenna. The beds of nails are covered with sheets. The hooks on which the wicked males and females hang—by their tongues for gossip, their hands for theft, their breasts for lechery, their feet for running after sin—are concealed behind screens. The piles of red-hot coals and icy snow onto which transgressors are flung are invisible that day. The angels of destruction have put away their fiery rods. The sinners who remain pious even in hell (there are such) go to a little synagogue where an iniquitous cantor intones the Sabbath prayers. The freethinkers (there are many of them in Gehenna) sit on logs and converse. As is usually the case with enlightened ones, their topic is how to improve their lot, how to make a better Gehenna.

That wintry late Sabbath afternoon a sinner named Yankel Farseer was saying: "The trouble with us in hell is that we are selfish: each sinner thinks only about his own business. If he believes that he can save his behind from a few lashes by the angel Dumah, he is in seventh heaven. If we could form a united front, we would not be in need of private intercession. We would come out with demands."

When he uttered the word "demands," his mouth began to water. He choked and puffed. Yankel was a fat man with broad shoulders, a round belly, short legs. He had long hair covering his bald spot and grew a beard—not a kosher beard as the pious have in paradise, but a rebellious one, every hair of which points at revolution.

One little delinquent, who braided his long hair in a ponytail tied with a wire he tore out of a bed of nails, asked, "What kind of demands, Comrade Yankel?"

"First, that the week in Gehenna should not last six days, but that we should have a four-day week. Second, that each villain get a six-week vacation, during which he may return to earth and break the Ten Commandments without being punished. Third, that we should not be kept away from our beloved sisters, the female sinners. We demand sex and free love. Fourth—"

"Dreams of a chopped-off head!" said Chaim Bontz, a former gangster. "The angel Dumah is not afraid of your demands and petitions. He does not even bother to read them."

"What do you propose?"

"The angels, like humans, understand only one thing—blows. We must arm ourselves. Rub out the angel Dumah, storm the court of heaven, break a few ribs among the righteous. Then we must take over paradise, Leviathan, the Wild Ox, the sanctified wine, all the other good things. Then—"

"Arm ourselves?" a petit bourgeois who had fallen into hell for swindling cried out. "Where will you get arms in hell? They don't give us a single knife or fork. The fiery coals we eat we have to pick up with our naked fingers. Besides, Gehenna does not last longer than a year except for Sabbaths and holidays. I am supposed to end my term on the day after Purim. If we begin a conspiracy now, the term may be prolonged. Do you know the punishment for conspiring against the angel Dumah?"

"This is the misfortune of us sinners," Yankel Farseer yelled out. "Everyone is only for himself. How about the wicked who will come after us? This year is not so bad yet, it has twelve months but next year will be a leap year."

"It is not my duty to worry about all the wicked in the world," replied the swindler. "I happen to be an innocent victim. All I did was forge a signature. I shed ink, not blood. Those who murder, set fire to houses and cause children to perish in the flames, those who stab and rape are not my brothers. If I were in charge here, I would keep them until the end of the six thousandth year!"

"Didn't I say that every sinner is out for himself?" Yankel Farseer spoke. "If we cannot unite, the angels can do to us as they please. In that case, why the idle talk? Let's play cards and finish out the rest of the Sabbath."

"Comrade Yankel," a sinner with eyeglasses spoke up, "may I say something?"

"Say. Talk doesn't change anything."

"My opinion is that we should concentrate mainly on culture. Before we come with maximal demands like six-week vacations with sex and free love, we must show the angels that we are sinners with spiritual goals. I propose that we publish a magazine."

"A magazine in Gehenna?"

"Yes, a magazine, and its name should be *The Gehennanik*. When you sign a petition, the angels take one look at it and they throw it away, or they blow their noses into it. But a magazine they would read. The righteous in paradise expire from boredom. They are overfed with the secrets of the Torah. They want to know what's going on in hell. They are curious about our view of the world, our way of thinking, our sex fantasies, and, most of all, they are intrigued by the fact that we are still atheists. A series of articles, 'The Atheists in Gehenna,' would become a smash hit in paradise. Of course, we would also publish a gossip column and a lot of special hell pornography. The saints would have something to enjoy and to complain about."

"Silly babble! I'm going to sleep." Chaim Bontz yawned.

"Who is going to do all this scribbling and how will this help us?" asked a sinner with a hoarse voice.

"You don't have to worry about who will do the writing," said the sinner with the eyeglasses. "We have a lot of writers here. I was a writer on earth myself. I was condemned to hell because I was supposed to be a rabble-rouser. Every Monday and Thursday, I changed my opinion. When it was profitable to preach Communism I became an ardent Communist and, likewise, I preached capitalism when that paid. They heaped accusations against me. But the fact is that I had many readers and they wrote me enthusiastic fan letters. It is true that I changed my opinions like gloves, but were my readers any more consistent? Here in hell—"

A sinner who looked young, and had long hair reaching down to his shoulders, asked, "Why publish a magazine? Why not open a theater? We have a shortage of paper here. Besides, it's so hot that the magazine will catch fire. The righteous are all half blind and don't understand our modern language and are not accustomed to our spelling. My advice is that we should organize a theatrical group."

"A theater in hell? Who's going to act? And who's going to attend? They punish us day and night."

"We will perform on Sabbaths and all holidays."

"Are there any scripts in Gehenna?"

"I have an idea for a play—a love affair between a sinner and a saint."

"What kind of love affair? The wicked and the saints never meet."

"I have thought it through thoroughly. My hero is lying on his bed of nails and screaming. He is an opera singer by profession and so wracked with pain that he breaks out into an aria. She, the saint, hears his song and falls madly in love with his voice. Then—"

"The saints in paradise are all deaf."

"This one happens not to be deaf."

"Well then, what follows?"

"To be able to meet him, she asks for permission from the angel Eshiel to dress up like a demon and to become one who dispenses lashes in Gehenna. Permission is granted, and so the two lovers meet. She is supposed to whip him, but when the angel Dumah looks away, she covers him with kisses and they soon reach a point where they cannot be one without the other."

"Melodrama of the worst kind!"

"What do you want to perform in Gehenna, *Migdal Oz* by Mosheh Chayim Luzzatto? Our sinners love action. A play like this would give the actors an opportunity to sing a song, to dance, and to make a couple of spicy jokes."

"Assuming that it works, what would the result be?"

"Theater is the best form of propaganda. It may very well be that the saints and the angels will visit our theater to see our plays. And between one act and the other, we would explain to them our point of view, our situation, and our philosophy."

"Your play is not realistic, and your plan is not realistic. Where will we perform—among the piles of coals? The saints will not come here. All day long they are busy with the secrets of the Torah and with munching Leviathan. In the evening they are afraid to leave paradise."

"What are they afraid of?"

"A couple of murderers and rapists managed to escape

from Gehenna. They prowl around at night. They have already killed several saints and have tried to ravish Sarah bas Tovim."

"This is the first time I've heard this."

"Of course, as long as we don't have any magazines, no one is informed about anything. The magazine would give us news and explain—"

"Fantasies, fantasies," a sinner who had been a politician on earth called out. "Culture will not solve our problem, and neither will the theater. What we really need is a progressive political party built on democratic principles. We don't need to come out with impossible demands, Comrade Yankel. We should be satisfied with a minimum. I have heard from a very reliable source that there is a liberal group among the angels who are asking for reforms in Gehenna."

"What kind of reforms?"

"They want us to have a five-day week. Besides Saturdays and holidays, we should be given a week's vacation in the World of Illusions. Some of them would request that the nails on the beds of nails should be two millimeters shorter. I was told that there is some change in their attitude toward homosexuality, lesbianism, and certainly masturbation. We could do a lot, but we need money."

"Money?" all the sinners called out with one voice.

"Yes, money. 'And money answereth all things,' Ecclesiastes has said. If we had money we could achieve everything without revolution, without petitions, without culture. In Gehenna as everywhere else everybody has his price. You are all greenhorns. I know Gehenna from top to bottom and inside out. With money we could even—"

The politician wanted to tell his listeners what else could be accomplished with money in Gehenna, but at that instant the Sabbath ended. The fires leaped up again. The nails on the beds began to glow with heat. The punishing demons grabbed up their rods, and a lashing and a whipping and a hanging and a wailing erupted once more. The politician who had just spoken about money winked an eye at one of the older demons and they both left—where they were going no one knew. Most probably to do some unkosher Gehenna business.

Translated by the author

The Last Gaze

THE NEWS of Bessie's death came as a shock from which he knew he would not easily recover. It was fifteen months since he'd last seen her, and only now did he realize how much she meant to him. That very night he went to the funeral parlor, but the girl at the window told him, "She isn't ready. Come back tomorrow morning."

He returned home and began a chess game with himself, making the moves for both sides. He tried smoking, but the tobacco tasted bitter. Although he hadn't eaten since breakfast, he felt bloated, as if he'd consumed a heavy meal. He stretched out on the sofa, leaving the lights on, and covered himself with his overcoat.

"If there is a hereafter," he mused, "let her appear before me now. Let her face become visible in the mirror, let her voice be heard, let some sign of her presence manifest itself." The lights shone with a midnight glare. The telephone on the nightstand remained silent. The radiator hissed and gurgled its last bit of steam. He imagined that he heard the movement of the earth as it rotated on its axis. That very second, as the earth spun amid the planets and fixed stars, multitudes of people and animals were giving up their lives. At least one hundred thousand men and women lay dying; many more would die the following day, and the next, and a week hence.

He partially covered his face with his hat, like a passenger on a train, and drifted into a half-sleep. He had brooded about his relationship with Bessie for years, but he could never explain it to himself. On the surface it appeared simple enough, but behind their mutual affection hovered a kind of enmity. They could neither stay together nor remain apart. Eventually they were able to get along only in the dark.

How had they spent their last night together, he wondered. How could they have known that this was to be their final meeting? What had they said to each other? What were the last words between them? Unfortunately, this last night had blended in his memory with many other nights. Most likely he'd promised to telephone the following day, but he never called her again, nor she him. Yet during those fifteen months he had thought of her every day, perhaps every hour. More than once he had put his hand on the receiver, and was about to lift it, but the power which had the final say ordained, No. Every time his telephone rang his hope soared that it was she. Then the day came when her brother called and told him the shattering news.

The radiator had grown still. Drowsily, he tried to

listen to his dreams, but there was nothing therein he
could grasp. The visions changed as quickly as they do
in a fever. In one dream he was in a narrow side street
somewhere. It was lined with wooden shacks, with roofs
like boys' caps, housing a race of dwarfs. In the middle
of the alley stood a straw bed stripped of linen. He lay
on this pallet and gave a tattered urchin, an occupant
of one of the huts, a dollar, with the understanding that
the boy was to change the bill and bring back ninety
cents in silver. But the boy never returned. "He's stolen
the dollar!" he berated himself, and deplored his stu-
pidity in having trusted the youngster. And mingled
with his regret was self-pity. What was he doing here
in a strange bed, in this forsaken alleyway far from
home, among a race of dwarfs? It all had to do with his
many failures.

He woke up. The clock showed a quarter past three.
He'd slept away half the night with nothing to show for
it but a senseless dream. Later he showered and shaved
and dressed in his finest suit. The previous day he'd
sent a huge wreath of flowers to the funeral parlor. He
was anxious to appear prosperous before Bessie's friends
and relatives. Carefully he chose his shirt, tie, and cuff
links. He prepared breakfast—not out of hunger, but
to avoid a drawn appearance. He brewed strong coffee,
added much sugar. Large flakes of snow were falling
outside and although it was the dead of winter, a fly
suddenly appeared. For a while it buzzed against the
windowpane, then landed near some crystals of spilled
sugar. It did not eat but seemed to ponder over them.
From time to time it entangled its back feet, then

straightened them out again. Finally, it landed on the brim of a saucer of leftover black coffee and gazed into it as if into an abyss. Perhaps, he had a sudden thought, the fly is Bessie.

He'd have to hurry. He wanted to see her alone, with no one looking on. The funeral parlor was not far from his house, but he took a taxi to avoid coming in from the cold with a red nose. Soon he was standing at the little window which connected the dead to the living.

"Fourth floor," the same girl told him.

He rode up on the elevator. The funeral parlor was deserted, an emptiness that would soon be overrun by a crowd. He stopped before a door with mottled milk-glass panels, which held a card bearing Bessie's name and the hour of her funeral. It seemed to him that, in some eerie fashion, Bessie had become an official with her own office and office hours. He pushed open the door and saw her coffin with a part of its lid removed. From the ceiling a colored lamp cast a pale light, which mixed with the daylight filtering through the stained-glass windows. He was alone with Bessie.

Her face was covered by a square piece of gauze. She seemed almost alive, only lovelier, a perfect portrait painted by a master who wished to protect it from the dust. She seemed to smile, the smile of someone about to wake up, who savors the last few moments of stolen sleep. Her hair was combed up in a net, her throat bound in a white collar like a nun's. Did she recognize him from under her closed lids? His heart pounded like a trip-hammer and his temples pulsated. Outwardly he remained placid, but he knew that he could not endure this tension long. He did a forbidden thing, hesitantly lifting up the gauze. He imagined that Bessie was aware of his gazing at her with enchantment and trepidation. He had uncovered her face like a bridegroom at the unveiling of the bride. Then he replaced the gauze, as if she were something sacred and forbidden to be looked at. Thus as a boy he used to steal a glimpse when the kohanim blessed the congregation.

Presently he heard footsteps, and another person opened the door. Someone else wanted a private look at Bessie. In his confusion, he brushed past the newcomer, and later he could not be sure whether it had been a man or a woman.

Downstairs he was told that the services would begin in a half hour. He went out into the street to avoid meeting any of Bessie's relatives. It was too cold and he was shivering, so he went into a luncheonette and ordered coffee. He warmed his hands on the cup, took a sip, and stared into the coffee as if expecting to discover in the hot fluid the solution to the riddle.

All the old altercations with Bessie, all the friction between them had vanished, leaving in their wake the pure love that had once been theirs. If only he could have looked at her a few moments longer! He sat there, drunk with the intoxication he had known from the very beginning with her. He was falling in love with her again, and it was no longer winter but the spring of twelve years ago. The snowflakes falling outside reminded him of blossoms; a blinding stream of sunlight filtered through a split in the overcast skies.

But it was too late. One could no longer cause Bessie

either good or evil. She lay there upstairs like a queen, independent of everyone, bestowing her grace equally upon all. He'd been prepared for every countermove in the chess game of love, except this. With one stroke she had checkmated him. In the wrinkles around her eyes and lips lingered an expression of triumph. He realized it only now: she had gained the upper hand completely. His heart pounded no longer but felt as if an unseen hand were squeezing it. He'd forgotten that one could lose absolutely. He hadn't reckoned with the kind of power that in one second erases everything petty and ambitious.

The clock in the coffee shop showed five minutes to eleven, and he went back to the funeral parlor. A crowd had gathered in the chapel. The coffin rested in its appointed place amid the wreaths of flowers. The electric candles were lit. All the benches were taken, save the last. Looking around, he saw unfamiliar faces. A woman sobbed with a laugh-like cry. A man honked his nose and wiped his spectacles. The women were whispering to one another, which reminded him of a women's synagogue during the Days of Awe. He sat down in an empty place. A rabbi in a tiny skullcap over a shock of freshly pomaded hair spoke with customary words, booming the biblical phrases with the usual mournful intonations: "He is the rock, His work is perfect: for all His ways are judgment: a God of truth and without iniquity, just and right is He." Afterward, the cantor chanted the prayer, "God is full of mercy." Dramatically, he switched from lulling whispers to an ear-shattering crescendo, and his chant, though obviously affected and rehearsed, tugged at the heart-strings, where grief and ceremony blend.

Afterward everyone stood up and began to file past the coffin to look at the corpse, as if for reassurance that they, the living, still possessed curiosity and strength. He did not join in this procession and went outside. The rabbi who had just concluded the eulogy was now matter-of-factly directing the cars, which had to maneuver in the narrow street to pick up mourners for the trip to the cemetery. The rabbi had forsaken his role as reverend and assumed the part of traffic expert, having cast off his solemnity like a mask.

For a while it appeared as if he, Bessie's friend, would be overlooked in the throng of mourners and bystanders, but one of the relatives spied him and directed him to a vacant seat in a limousine. He sat in the car among strangers. A man and a woman talked interminably about a lost key to her apartment, and the dire consequences of having lost it on a Sunday, when they'd been unable to locate a locksmith and had been forced to pierce the metal door with an electric drill. The relating of this incident did not exhaust the topic. The lost key became the theme of the trip. All the passengers offered up similar happenings, their own and their neighbors'.

He sat there astounded. Why had they bothered to come to the funeral at all, with so little respect for the deceased? Or was this a way to forget and ignore death while facing it? Such callousness in itself was an enigma. He pressed his face against the pane. He wanted to disassociate himself from these people. The car hurtled through the wilds of Brooklyn, through streets and avenues so strange they might as well have been in Philadelphia or Chicago. The Sunday quiet made them even uglier and more desolate than on a weekday.

They rode past a vast cemetery, a city of graves. The tombstones resembled a forest of toadstools, extending as far as the eye could see. Here and there among the crosses loomed the statue of an angel, its wings laden with snow, sorrow in its blind eyes. The living had in some mysterious fashion poured their fears and regrets into the stone and remained hollow shells themselves.

After a while, the limousine turned into the cemetery. Everything had been prepared beforehand: the open grave, the artificial grass, which did not even pretend to create an illusion. A woman cried out. Some man said Kaddish, reading the Aramaic words transliterated into English on a leaflet printed especially for such occasions. What he witnessed was not just a burial but an ancient sacrifice wherein a lot was cast to determine who should be given back to the soil on this gloomy winter day. They had to fill the grave in a hurry, before the earth froze.

As soon as the ceremony was over, the rush to depart began. Everyone spoke of one thing only—the best way to get back to the city. The matter of transportation had now become the paramount issue; men and women vied with one another in their knowledge of shortcuts, tunnels, and bridges.

He did not return to the limousine but struck out on his own, in search of a bus or subway. He had severed his relations with those who drove back in the black Cadillac with the stiff chauffeur. Someone had to acknowledge that Bessie was now lying in a casket covered with earth, while myriads of microbes were beginning to decompose her flesh and return it to the elements. Did some vestige of thought still remain in her brain? Had her spirit been entirely extinguished, and did absolute darkness alone hold sway? If that were so, Bessie hadn't even died—she had just vanished. It was actually his funeral, he thought, not hers.

He shivered and raised his collar as he trudged through snow and slush. He lifted his eyes heavenward; perhaps he would be given a sign there. Maybe the divine powers would make an exception. But the clouds overhead writhed brown as rust. The wind caught up his hat, but he recovered it at the very last second. The Lord of the Universe, or His appointees delegated to rule this insignificant planet, were apparently in no mood for revelation.

As he sloshed down the street, a hodge-podge of garages, unoccupied buildings, and empty lots, a horn sounded. He turned to see a man leaning out of a car window who said, half questioningly, "You were at the funeral. You want to go back to the city?"

"Yes."

"Get in." He got in and thanked the stranger. Only now did he take a real look at the driver, elderly but powerfully built, with broad shoulders, gray curly hair, and a red flattened face with a wide nose and thick lips clamped around a cigar. His eyes were gray and over-hung by bristling brows. He wore a snappy yellowish overcoat of the kind worn by old people attempting to appear younger. His hat sat jauntily on his head, sporting a red feather in its band. Even his manner of driving accentuated his efforts to appear young: he lounged in his seat, holding the wheel negligently in one hand, with the easiness of a driver fully capable of handling any possible emergency. As he drove along, he spoke to his passenger, turning the edge of his profile carelessly in the process.

"Well, she is no longer with us," he said both to himself and to the passenger.

"Yes."

"A remarkable woman. There aren't many like her." And he pressed the car horn, barely missing a pedestrian.

For a time he maintained a morbid silence. Then he said, "I know you. That is, not personally, but Bessie told me all about you. She showed me your picture. That's how I recognized you."

"Are you a relative?"

"No, hardly that. We got to know each other about a year ago, and right off it turned, so to speak, into a friendship. She held nothing back, told me all there was to know, and I respected her for it. What's the point in bluffing? No one would expect a woman her age to be a virgin."

He abruptly braked the car for a red light. For a while neither of them spoke. Then the driver began again: "What was it that happened between you two? Why didn't you get married? —But like I say, it's all fate. There is nothing one can do to forestall destiny. I wanted her to come to some sort of a decision. I'm not rich, mind you, but she would have had a good life with me. Both my daughters are married. I'm in real estate. I build bungalows. If I wanted to, I could retire today. I offered to take her to Europe, to Israel, wherever she wanted. My sons-in-law don't need my money and you can't take it with you, so why the hell save and skimp? But she kept putting it off, putting it off. —*Hey, where do you think you're going?*" he suddenly yelled to a passerby. "*You damned bum!*"

For a time he was silent. "Do you smoke? I smoke ten cigars a day. The doctors say it's bad for a man of my age, but one thing is sure, I won't die young anymore. And as long as I live, I want to enjoy myself. Once you're on the other side, it's already too late. Yes sir, it looked as if Bessie and I would hit it off real fine until that other party horned in—"

"The *other* party?"

"That Levy guy. She didn't tell you? I was under the impression that you'd remained friends."

"No, she didn't tell me."

"Yes, the dentist. What she saw in him I'll never know, but what do we men know about women's taste? He talks real fancy and runs to concerts at Carnegie Hall. He is also some kind of a big shot with the Zionists or whoever they are. As soon as I heard about him I warned her. She introduced us and asked my opinion. I'm the sort of guy, if I liked him, I'd have said so. I'm like that in business, too. Somebody can be my biggest competitor, but if they turn out a nice piece of work I'll be the first to admit it. But I didn't like him, so I told her, 'Do what you like, we'll still be friends.' And from that time on she started to go down. I called her a few times after that, but she didn't call me back. I took her out, too, to the theater, a restaurant. I was ready to forgive and forget, but she was proud. Too proud. She said to me, 'Sam, it's the end of me.' I said, 'Why is it the end?' She said, 'When others don't respect me I don't care, but when I lose my self-respect, then it's the finish.' What happened was, that sneaky little dentist went back to his wife because her father had died and left her a bundle. I found out that during the time he was going out with Bessie he kept a mistress, some Mrs. Rothstein, a divorcee. He is one of those guys who flit from woman to woman and think they deceive the whole world. What did she ever see in him? It wasn't love—she loved only you. But there is such a thing as ambition. Especially in women. —*Where is he going, that bum? Why do they give people like that a license?* —Yes, ambition. She was ready to marry and he, as they say, pulled the wool over her eyes. You didn't see her the last few months?"

"No."

"Well, she was crushed. Completely crushed. A good woman, a noble woman. How was it you didn't call her?"

"It just happened that way."

"I understand. I know how it is. He was at the funeral today, too, the little quack. He sat right in the first row and acted like the number-one mourner. He tried to

source, he had fallen into the hands of these adversaries of God.

Naamah brought him into her chamber, and even though it was dark, he could see her bed and a huge man lying in it. It was Ashiel, a fallen angel, one of the sons of Anak, the giant men of renown. Naamah introduced Methuselah to him, saying, "Here is one of my oldest lovers," and the other one asked, "Are you Methuselah? She speaks about you all the time. She craves you, not me. Even though I am a giant and you are as small as a locust."

"He is small, but he is a real man," Naamah said. "While your semen is like water and foam."

"I will go now," Ashiel said, "to the men of wisdom in our assembly."

Ashiel left, and Methuselah embraced Naamah and he came into her. She revealed to him secrets of heaven and earth. "Your father, Enoch," she said, "became Yahweh's head of the angels, the Lord Metatron. Actually, he is nothing but His servant. Your son Lamech is among the shadows of Dumah." Naamah revealed to Methuselah that her mother, Zillah, was a harlot and she lay with all her husband's friends as well as with his enemies. She begot her, Naamah, from one of Adah's sons, Jubal, the ancestor of all who play the lyre and pipe. Naamah continued to say to Methuselah, "Let it be known to you that Yahweh's world is nothing but a madhouse. He has erred by creating man, and he commanded your grandson, Noah, to build an ark to save himself and his household and all the animals from the flood. But be sure that the flood will never come upon the earth. Here in the netherworld an assembly of wise men from all over the world is meeting. They came from Kush and from India, from Sodom and from Nineveh, from Shinar and Gomorrah. Yahweh is old and tired. He thinks He is the only God and is forever jealous of other gods, constantly in dread that His own angels might rebel against Him and take dominion of the universe. We, the demons of this generation, are young and many. Yahweh threatens to open the windows of heaven and bring the flood. But we have scholars who have discovered how to close them. In all these years when you, Methuselah, lived with your faithful wives and concubines, plowed the fields by the sweat of your brow, and attended your flocks of sheep, many men of learning sprang forth. They can split hairs, count the sand of the sea, the eyes of a fly, measure the stench of a skunk and the venom of a snake. Some of these men have learned to tame crocodiles and spiders, they can make the old young, the fools wise, and reverse the sexes. They can reach the very depths of perversion. Stay with us, Methuselah, and you will be twice as clever and ten times as virile."

Naamah kissed Methuselah and caressed him. She said, "Yahweh had only one wife, the Shekinah, and for countless years they have been separated because of His impotence and her frigidity. He has forbidden all deeds which bring pleasure to men and women, such as theft, murder, adultery. Even the sweet coveting of another man's wife He considers a crime. But here we have turned teasing and tantalizing into the highest art. Come with me, Methuselah, and I will take you to the assembly of the wise which gathered here and you will witness their accomplishments and hear what they intend to do in the happy time to come. My lover, Ashiel, is there now and many fallen angels who became weary of the daughters of Adam and now lie one with the other. If you stay with me I will give you all my maids and many of the imps for our common delight."

Methuselah and Naamah rose and she took him through a labyrinth of many passages. They entered a temple where each scholar was speaking about his land and its people.

A sage of Sodom told the gathering that they were teaching children in Sodom the art of manslaughter, as well as the arts of arson, embezzlement, lying, robbery, treachery, the abuse of the old and the rape of the young. A glutton from Nineveh was telling how to eat the flesh of animals while they are still alive and to suck their blood in its flow. Prizes were awarded to the most accomplished thieves, robbers, forgers, liars, whores, torturers, as well as to sons and daughters who dishonored their parents and to widows who had excelled in poisoning their husbands. They had established special courses for blasphemy, profanity, and perjury. The great Nimrod himself was teaching cruelty to animals.

An old demon by the name of Shavriri was giving an oration and saying, "Yahweh is a God of the past, but we are the future. Yahweh is dying or perhaps already dead, but the serpent is alive and giving birth to countless new serpents by copulating with our queen, Lilith, and the ladies of her co irt. The angels in heaven have all been blinded by the curse of light, but we will bring back the primeval darkness, which is the substance of all matter."

Harsh music was being played for the assembly, and the singing was so loud it pierced Methuselah's ears. He could not tell the difference anymore between laughter and crying, the cheering of female demons and the wild cries of male hobgoblins. "I'm too old for all this revelry," Methuselah was saying, not knowing whether he spoke to himself or to Naamah. He fell on his knees and pleaded with her to take him back to his tent, to his bed, to the bliss of old age and rest. For the first time in almost a thousand years, the fear of the grave had left him. He was ready to embrace the angel of death with his sharp sword and myriad eyes.

The next morning when the servant girl brought Methuselah a bowl with date juice she found him dead. The news spread that the oldest man on earth had returned to dust. Noah soon learned that his grandfather had died, but he could not leave his wife and his three sons, Shem, Ham, and Japheth, as well as the ark which the Almighty had told him to build. God's decision to release the flood was about to take place. The windows of heaven began to open and no one could close them. All the lords of Sodom and Shinar, Nineveh and Admah were about to be swept away in the deluge. Somewhere in the depths of Dumah and Sheol a bevy of devils were hiding, Naamah among them. Methuselah knew the past quite well and he had gotten a glimpse of the future. God had taken a perilous risk when He created man and gave him dominion over all other creatures of the earth, but He was about to promise by the rainbow in the clouds never again to bring a flood and destroy all flesh. It became clear to Him that all punishment was in vain, since flesh and corruption were the same from the very beginning and always will remain the scum of creation, the very opposite of God's wisdom, mercy, and splendor. God had granted the sons of Adam an abundance of self-love, the precarious gift of reason, as well as the illusions of time and space, but no sense of purpose or justice. Man would manage somehow to crawl upon the surface of the earth, forward and backward, until God's covenant with him ended and man's name in the book of life was erased forever.

Translated by the author